Junglee Girl

by

GINU KAMANI

aunt lute books
SAN FRANCISCO

First Edition
10 9 8 7 6 5 4 3 2 1

Aunt Lute Books
PO Box 410687
San Francisco, CA 94141

This book was funded in part by a grant from the National Endowment for the Arts.
This is a work of fiction. In no way does it intend to represent any real person, living or dead, or any real incidents.
"Maria" and "Waxing The Thing" first appeared in *Our Feet Walk the Sky: Women of the South Asian Diaspora*, ed. The Women of South Asian Descent Collective (San Francisco: Aunt Lute Books, 1993).

Cover Art: "Nayika" by Gogi Saroj Pal
Cover and Text Design: Pamela Wilson Design Studio
Typesetting: JBWiley, Drago Design

Senior Editor: Joan Pinkvoss
Managing Editor: Christine Lymbertos

Production: Cristina Azócar   Jee Yeun Lee
                       Vita Iskandar   Kathleen Wilkinson

Production Support: Jonna K. Eagle   Melissa Levin
                       Jamie Lee Evans   Michelle Uribe
                       Irma de Jesus   Alexa Weinstein

Printed in the U.S.A. on acid-free paper.

Library of Congress Cataloging-in-Publication Data

Kamani, Ginu, 1962–
    Junglee Girl / by Ginu Kamani
        p.   cm.
    ISBN 1-879960-41-9 — ISBN 1-879960-40-0 (pbk.)
    1. Short Stories, Indic (English)   2. Social problems—Fiction.
    3. Women—India—Social Life and customs—Fiction.   4. Women—India—
    –Social conditions—Fiction.   5. United States—Social conditions—
    –Fiction.   I. Title.
    PR9497.32.K36   1995
    823——dc20   94-46891
                                                            CIP

For my junglee muses:

Ma and Dad

Priya

David

Table of Contents

Ciphers

The woman claiming the berth across from mine in the train compartment must have been my age, but she looked older, more self-important. She had the red mark of the auspicious married woman in her hair parting and three young children to prove her fertility. She stopped her children from sitting on the long hard seat, motioning them to wait.

"It's dirty," she scolded them in Gujarati, pointing to the dull green vinyl which had worn away in parts to reveal the coarse padding underneath. She reached into her oversized plastic shopping bag, pulling out a printed cotton bedspread that she snapped open with a quick flick of her wrists. She covered the seat and tucked the edges in. The woman nodded in satisfaction, patted her hair into place, then sat down and lifted the three children up beside her so they sat propped up against the seat back. The four of them sat squashed against each other in the middle of the seat, with ample room on either side.

The train whistle blew, and the tea and snack vendors who droned their wares by the windows suddenly switched into high gear, running from one window to the next, shouting out Hot tea! Hot tea...! Fresh puri-bhaji...! Hot samosas! Thin porters in bright red shirts raced by with tottering mounds of baggage balanced on their heads. I was sitting on an Indian train for the first time in a decade, but the scene was just as I remembered it from childhood. The big difference was that, this time, I was traveling alone.

The train slowly pulled out of the station. The woman across from me looked at me then for the first time. In her quick look, she took in my short hair, my knee-length dress and ringless third finger. Her evaluation made, she avoided my eyes. She looked over my head, through my feet, at the door and windows, but not into my eyes. Though her children were staring at me, through a series of subtle cues from their mother, they had understood that I was to be given the silent treatment.

I remembered being that young age, and staring at strangers in that same fascinated way, knowing that they were humans like us, but knowing that they were not from our family. If, by some chance, it was determined that these strangers were friends of friends, or hailed from our parents' natal villages, or were otherwise established as people of good family, then the ice would break quickly, and food would be offered from both sides, followed by the sharing of board games or card games or amusing pastimes like guessing the names of Hindi film songs. But until then, the adults sat stone-faced and the children stuck to their own.

The young mother across from me spoke to her children in a shrill Gujarati punctuated by such endearments as greedy, idiot, blackie and pig. The children were obviously used to these mocking asides and did not respond. But it had been years since I had heard those insults spoken with such fluency, and I was immediately flooded with memories of shouting matches when our group of young cousins would exhaust the usual English insults: You stupid! You idiot! Fool! Crackpot!, all of which had a peculiar weightiness that would quickly tire us out. But then we would switch to our reservoir of delicious Gujarati insults: Pig! Monkey! Cockroach! Elephant!, and somehow these abuses from our mother tongue were so much more raucous and full of abandon that they elevated us back into good humor and collaborative play.

Giggles rose up in me like bubbles as the woman chided her children. I stifled the first few, but I couldn't help but smile when the woman called her son a goat, and I finally had to guffaw and cough when she called her daughter a donkey. The woman looked up at me sharply and I pressed my twitching lips shut.

She opened her mouth to speak, but then turned and frowned at the window, unsure of whether to engage with me. After all, I was a stranger, and it was probably best not to get involved. But then as I snorted and cleared my throat again, she took a deep breath and sat forward.

"You are Christian?" she snapped. I shook my head apologetically. She looked pointedly at my dress, or frock, as she would have referred to it.

"You are Muslim from Delhi?" She was still cross.

"No," I replied politely.

"You are Madrasi," she sneered.

"No. I've never been to Madras."

"Then you must be Punjabi," she taunted.

I smiled faintly. She was bent on pinning me down.

"Where you are from?" she rasped.

"From right here in Bombay," I said sweetly. She nodded and waved her hand.

"Now I know. You are Malayali." She looked away, signaling that the discussion was over. But from the corner of her eye she saw me shake my head.

"Maharashtrian," she continued emphatically. She straightened the pleats of her sari.

I stared at her. I was suddenly aware of feeling hurt. If she weren't so prejudiced by my short hair and western dress, and the quickly made assumption that I was unmarried and childless, she would surely have seen right away that I was Gujarati. I opened my book and began reading to signal that the conversation really was over.

"I know a girl from Goa who looks just like you."

I turned the page and crossed my legs, settling into my stance.

"But naturally you are Bengali." She turned to her children and nodded sagely.

Suddenly I tired of her game and decided to burst her bubble. I reached into my purse and pulled out a package of Gluco biscuits. I tore the wrapper slowly, to make sure that I had the attention of all three children. They looked at me hungrily.

"Biscuit aapu?" I asked in Gujarati and held out the pack to the older boy.

The woman gasped in horror and slapped down her son's outstretched hand.

"You're Gujarati!" she howled in rage. She was so offended by this realization that she instinctively reached back and covered her head with her sari for protection.

"Yes, auntie," I said in wide-eyed sing-song. "I am a pukka Gujarati."

All three children were staring at me slack-jawed. Their mother slapped each one quickly across the mouth. She shouted at them. "How many times have I told you not to take things from strangers, huh? Have you no shame? Sit up straight and keep your hands to yourselves!"

I put down my book and looked at the woman fumbling for her handkerchief with shaking hands.

"Are you also Gujarati?" I asked with a smile.

She pursed her lips and looked out of the window. Her fingers twisted the handkerchief into a tense rope.

"We are the real Gujaratis, from *Gujarat!*" she spat.

"My family is from Saurashtra," I said gently. "We are Jains."

Her face turned pale and her brow knitted furiously.

"These days anybody can say they come from anywhere," she muttered in exasperation. "I'm not so stupid that I will believe everything!"

She pushed her children out of the way and stretched out on the seat. She crossed her arms tightly over her chest and pressed her lips shut. She stared pointedly at the miniature ceiling fan. The three youngsters re-seated themselves timidly by the window, looking at each other nervously. Their mother was now in a bad mood, and any disturbance was likely to result in a hard slap across the head. Even though I was Gujarati, I was obviously a trouble-maker if I had caused their mother to reach this state.

The first time I realized that there were others besides Gujaratis in the world was when my oldest cousin married a Punjabi woman. My cousin had returned from studying "abroad" and announced to the family that he was now a married man. The adults were shocked to hear that *she* was Punjabi. That made her completely different! There was much grumbling among the women of the family about having to cope with *her* on top of all their countless chores.

We children could tell she was completely different because she laughed a lot and gave us lots of sweets and kisses every time we went to her room to visit her. Her kisses left big red splotches on our faces which we gigglingly rubbed off each other. She dressed in chiffon saris printed with dazzling sunflowers, roses, hibiscus. She let the saris fall carelessly across her bosom instead of securing them at the shoulder with pins. She wore tight blouses that were always on the verge of bursting, and didn't mind in the least if we barged in on her while she was dressing. She wore her hair short, with an enormous red bindi moistly spreading between her eyebrows. And to top it all, she had the most daring collection of sunglasses we had ever seen.

This woman was *not* Gujarati, most especially with her given name of Lajinder. My grandmother, matriarch of the household, quite firmly changed Lajinder's name to Lakshmi, after the goddess of wealth and prosperity. After all Lakshmi bhabhi hailed from a very wealthy family and should bring a considerable dowry to her husband's home, even if the newlyweds had joined in a "love marriage." For many months there was an angry stand-off in the house between my grandmother and Lakshmi, as Lakshmi refused to negotiate any dowry from her family. During those early months, every morning Lakshmi would perform the young wife's duty of massaging my grandmother's feet, but she did it wearing the lowest-cut blouses, the tightest dresses and the flimsiest nightgowns, kneeling dutifully at my grandmother's feet so that the old woman was forced to look at Lakshmi's bouncing breasts, or hold her head high and look away. One morning my grandmother had had enough and she burst into tears, wailing to god to release her from the torments of her life. From then on, all talk of the dowry ceased, and Lakshmi dressed far more modestly in our family home.

For all the ease with which Lakshmi bhabhi picked up the Gujarati language and followed every Gujarati custom concerning food, cleanliness and finances set up by our family, she was never ever considered Gujarati. She was always referred to as "that Punjabi." There was an invisible line that she was not allowed to cross, even after she had become one of the most powerful women in our family. For me, the very fact that she would never turn into a Gujarati made her my favorite female relative. I couldn't really explain why.

I sat on the train wondering about my clothes. I was wearing a printed rayon dress and closed shoes. I wore no jewelry other than my silver hoop earrings and my nondescript watch. I had eyeliner around my eyes and a little petroleum jelly on my lips. Would I have gone unnoticed in a sari or salwar-khameez?

I walked out of the compartment into the swaying corridor of the train. I slowly walked past all the compartments in the ladies' section, looking at how the women were dressed. Rich, poor, thin, fat, none of them resembled me. It wasn't just that none of them wore a dress, but that all of them looked at me with burning eyes, without recognition. I walked back to my berth and sat by the window. I watched my reflection in the dusty window pane, superimposed on the dazzling green fields that stretched out to the horizon.

I thought about how and where I directed my gaze when evaluating an unknown woman. Whenever possible, I always looked directly at the eyes and mouth first, then at the rest of the face, and only then would I attempt to integrate the woman's clothing with what was expressed in her face. My guess was that even in a sari, or other traditional Indian clothes, something in my eyes, and the set of my mouth, would give me away, would mark me as other, outsider, oblique.

The second non-Gujarati whom I remember being aware of was my Maharashtrian ayah, or bai. She was most certainly different, because she wore her sari in the traditional Maharashtrian manner, the long material pulled through her legs and out the other side and tucked in at the back of the waist in such a way that her buttocks were perfectly outlined. This way of wearing the sari was similar to how Indian men wear the traditional dhoti, but somehow the material stretching taut between the legs of the men never outlined anything quite as interesting as my bai's wonderful hips. As a young girl I never thought about her body consciously, but every time she walked by me, I was drawn to look at her shapely quivering flesh.

Neither the Gujarati style nor the North Indian style of wearing the sari allowed for the outlining of any sensuous shapes below the waist. Thus, in my childish imagination, it was only Maharashtrian women servants who had buttocks. As I visited the houses of my Gujarati friends, most of whom also had bais working for them, I came to have an appreciation for the various kinds of sari-wrapped buttocks that jiggled and sweated on the hips of our bais. Eventually my friends and I realized that we could do our bai-watching in the park, where dozens of these women came during the evening, bringing their young charges to play on the swings and slides.

These bais were definitely not Gujarati. They were too different! No matter that in some Gujarati households the Maharashtrian bais had worked there for decades and spoke only Gujarati, ate only Gujarati food and regaled their gods with only Gujarati bhajans.

Wearing their saris the way they did, there was no question of these bais ever becoming one of us.

After all my years in America, my being Gujarati had lost its potency. In the West, I was Indian. Nothing further. In India, we had never been *Indian*. Though the word India was used everywhere all the time, "Indian" was used so rarely in my early years that the American term cowboys and Indians entered our vocabulary unchallenged. The only uses of Indian I can remember from my early years were from the radio reports of the steadily advancing Indian Army during the 1971 war with Pakistan, and from the title of the English-language newspaper, *The Indian Express*.

Sitting on the train, watching the Gujarati woman carefully avoiding me, I wondered if my retort to her angry attempt at pinning me down should simply have been, *I'm Indian!* She would have looked at me blankly. On top of everything, the woman might have wondered, is this insolent girl so stupid as to imagine that I can't see that she is from this country? My dark skin, hair and eyes made me visibly Indian. On the other hand, if I had been light-skinned, there might have been some doubt about my identity, and consequently, less of a need to judge me harshly.

That reminded me of where else the term Indian had come up in my youth. It was to describe yet another non-Gujarati, a Kashmiri girl, who was appraised by my mother as being so fair-skinned that she definitely did not look Indian. This was my friend Radha, who looked exactly like a doll, with her curly brown hair and eerie hazel eyes. Her eyebrows were sparse golden arcs, unlike my black ones that almost met in the center of my forehead; her lips were light pink, unlike my dark purple ones. I didn't see any of this until my mother pointed it out. To me, Radha was exactly like a doll, a foreign doll. I wanted nothing more than to play with her.

Radha had the most benevolent nature of any child I knew. She was always mentally alert but quiet, always ready for action but motionless. She would do anything I wanted her to do. She would lift up her dress for me, higher and higher, until her entire gleaming white torso was revealed, right up to the sloping pink nipples. I would shout, "Simon Says, keep your hands in the air!" and she would stand rigid for minutes on end with her face hidden behind her upturned dress.

I would walk up to her and lightly dig my finger into her bellybutton. She would sigh, but not laugh. Then I would walk behind her and wedge her hand-sewn white panties in between her buttocks. She would clench the muscles as I touched her, then relax them. Then I would order, "Simon Says, hold your dress up with one hand and pull your chuddis off with the other!" And Radha would willingly oblige by pushing her panties down with one hand and squirming and kicking out of them. Then I would kneel down and tense my forearm and push Radha's thighs apart. Radha would slide onto my arm. She was so small, I could stand up and lift her into the air, where she balanced gracefully on my limb, her naked legs tautly extended like those of a tiptoeing ballerina, her head lost in the flying flounces of her tutu.

Radha was not Gujarati. She did not even have to be Indian if she didn't want. All around her were adults and children who would help her take on any fantasy identity she wanted. When Radha did occasionally speak, she made it clear that when she grew up she was going to be a famous actress in Hollywood. The adults loved this vision of Radha as performer. Such a light-skinned girl should definitely be put on show. I wasn't quite sure how Radha the doll would grow into Radha the Hollywood film star, but when at a private film screening in Bombay I saw an American actress in the nude for the first time, I noticed immediately the small pink nipples that glowed on her breasts, and realized that Radha would fit right in.

The rocking and rumbling of the train has put the three children to sleep. The woman is now sitting up, reading a Gujarati paperback. She looks at me occasionally with long frowning stares, then returns to her book. When I return her look, it is many long seconds before she looks away. She has steeled herself against both my strangeness and my familiarity. She acknowledges my presence, but there is nothing about me that she wants to know. The persistent unabashed flood of questions that is the mark of curious Indians will not pass her lips. So we sit in amicable silence in the cramped quarters of the train. We can finish our long journey in peace.

I could have told the Gujarati woman that I was Brazilian, Mexican, or even Ethiopian, just a few of the identities commonly ascribed to me by hopeful strangers in the U.S. I could have claimed to be Israeli, Egyptian or Turkish; even Italian, Spanish, Portuguese. That is the beauty of being Gujarati. The ports of Gujarat have been active centers of trade for millennia, and have attracted not only Arabs, Turks, Mongols, Persians, Greeks, Romans and Africans, but then later also the English, Spanish, French and Portuguese, all of whose genes have mingled over centuries with the original inhabitants of Gujarat so that even we Gujaratis are fooled by each other.

I want to take the face of the woman between my hands and tell her gently, so as not to scare her: Don't you know that there are Gujaratis in every country on earth now? Don't you know that our culture has caused subtle shifts in every community, and in turn, every community is subtly shifting the Gujaratis?

I intensify my stare and try to blaze a telepathic message into her frowning brow: It doesn't matter anymore what identity I was born into.

She melts a little under my stare, her face softening into concern. I lean forward and breathe deeply as I imagine conveying the ultimate: What matters is that I am *sexual*.

She puts her book down and looks at me languidly through drooping lashes. I frame the last of my message, wishing she would read me like her book: Being sexual has reshaped my knowledge, my feelings, my very breath. *That* is what fools you; that is what you turn away from in *yourself* when you turn away from me.

The Gujarati woman remains unmoved by my secrets. She leans forward and slides shut the compartment door. Then she reaches behind her and quickly undoes the tightly coiled bun at the nape of her neck. She shakes free her long hair and runs her fingers slowly down the length of it, head bowed to one side.

I am shocked, as I always am to see how sensuality abruptly descends on the sternest of Indian women when they loosen their thick dark hair. With her hair down, this smug judgmental mother of three is suddenly so breathtakingly beautiful that I want to cry. She looks at me slyly, conspiratorially, savoring the feel of her long tresses between her fingers.

"Why don't you grow your hair," she murmurs. "Long hair looks so good on us, don't you think?"

She pushes up her window as high as it will go. The wind lifts her hair around her like a lone hawk suspended on a bank of air. Her hair spreads out, shading her, like the flat top of a solitary baobab tree. If only I could climb into those silken branches...

An old familiar longing rushes into my throat, hammering at my vocal chords, drying me out with desire. I know this woman. I know her well. She is part of my recurring dream of coming home to India to be greeted by thousands of women running down a hill with their long hair swooping behind them like black garlands of welcome, like black birds released from captivity to honor my return.

I feel the slow uncoiling in my groin as the heat of my many tightly held selves burns through me. Resistance I'm not aware of holding suddenly snaps, and the train compartment, the woman, her sleeping children, the rusted ceiling fan, the tracks, the fields, the hazy sky, spin me so fiercely that I have to lean back and let it all rock through me. The brooding, dreaming girl I had been ten years earlier, wanting to be embraced and ensnared and embodied by these ciphers of women that surrounded me, has become a brooding, dreaming adult, still aching to decipher, derange, delight. I need to start over: I require once again a pliant will, a chameleon identity, and the reconfigured time of cycles and sieves that runs me aground again and again in a rut of meaningless circumstances, but then suddenly drops me right down the trap door of surface and superfice into the rushing female river below.

I feel the hair on my head jumping and growing and the hem of my dress lengthening and unfolding, drawing me closer to home.

Lucky Dip

During the lunch hour at school, I stayed in the classroom with the few girls who didn't like playing catch or the statue game L-O-N-D-O-N in the courtyard. We would gather together and exchange our lunches: jam and butter rolls, French toast, cucumber and tomato sandwiches with the crusts cut off, curry rice...Eventually we would tire of toying with our tiffins, snap them shut and pull a few desks and chairs together in a circle. It was up to me to think of a game to play.

Simi would start. "Maya, why are you sitting so quietly? We know you have something up your sleeve." We called her Simi bomb-bomb, because she was the only one in our class of ten-year-old girls who had a big bosom and wore a bra. Her uniforms were all shorter in the front because now they had to climb over her chest.

It was too hot to sit on the floor and play pick-up sticks or five stones. It was too boring to line up at the windows and call to the half-and-half hijras under the bridge. The hijras bathed in the open like men, but then hid behind a torn bedsheet to put on their saris and makeup. They couldn't really hear us, but the school principal in her office could hear us clearly. She would send our class teacher, Billy Goat, up from the staff room to tie us to our chairs. But her hands would shake so hard that the lunch break would be over by the time she finished tying us up.

Mumtaz said shyly, "I saw the new Shashi Kapoor film yesterday. He is so cute!" Mumtaz was in love with all the male movie stars.

"Massive crush! Massive crush!" The girls burst into chiding sing-song. Mumtaz saw every new Hindi movie that was released. Her mother always took her. Sometimes she saw six movies a week. Her family was very rich and they lived in a huge mansion. Mumtaz had no time for studies.

"Hey Mu-mu," cried Hema. "I heard they're going to hire a new teacher to teach us Maths. A man! He has a big pouf on his head and keeps his shirt buttons open till *here!*" Hema squealed with delight. "Poor Mu-mu, how will you cope!"

"Massive crush! Massive crush!" The girls started again, banging on the desks.

"But if we get a new teacher for Maths then where will DeSouza go?"

"To the mental hospital, where she belongs!"

"All right, all right!" I interrupted. This could go on for hours.

"I have something." I cracked each knuckle one by one, and looked intently at the group.

"Want to play N-P-A-T?"

NamePlaceAnimalThing. We scrambled for paper, pencils, rulers. We columned and titled our game sheets. We huddled together as I jabbed out the call: "Hip dip dip, my blue ship, sailing in the water, like a cup and saucer, hip dip dip. Okay, it falls on me. I'll start the alphabet." We were ready to begin.

"A! bcdefghijklmnop..."

"Stop!"

"Q."

"But you said P!"

"I know I said P, but I was already on Q. Stop arguing and play. Ready? Go!"

Four columns, *Name, Place, Animal, Thing*, four items all beginning with Q. Place was easy: Quebec, Queensland, Qatar. Thing was okay: quill, quilt, question mark. Animal: quail...I coughed and looked around. The other girls hurried to cover their sheets, but I saw that every one of them was stumped.

"Okay, I'm ready!"

They could see me smirking. I began the count.

"One...two...three..."

"Stop going so fast!" They were biting their pencils.

"...six...seven...eight..."

"God, slow down, stop cheating."

"Okay, okay, but it won't do you any good. Seven...eight...nine...ten. Stop! Put your pencils down, take your hands off the page, don't try anything funny. Start from the end. Mumtaz, Hema, Sadhana, Milly, Simi, me. Go. Thing."

"I have quill..."

"Ya, me too..."

"...quilt..."

"...quilt..."

"...quill..."

"I have quadrant, so ten points for me, five for the rest of..."

"What do you mean you have quadrant? Who said it's a thing?"

"Quadrant is a noun, a common noun, not a proper noun, and common nouns are things, so quadrant is a thing. I get ten points, quill gets five, quilt gets five. Next."

"Eh, don't cheat Maya, we all know how you like to cheat."

"Next! Animal. Mumtaz, your turn."

"I couldn't think of anything. There's no animal that begins with Q!"

"Quail, you stupid. Everybody knows quail begins with Q."

"Oh god, I completely forgot."

"Tough luck. So everyone who has an answer gets extra points. Hema?"

"I have quail..."

"...quail..."

"...quail..."

"...quail..."

"I have quagga, so I get..."

"What?! I swear Maya, you're always making up..."

"...just see how she spells it..."

"...hate playing with Maya, always cheating..."

"Quagga, don't you know? Where's your dictionary? Go home and look it up. It's extinct. So, quail gets ten points and quagga gets twenty. Next one? Place."

"I have Queensland."

"...Queensland..."

"...Queensland..."

"...Quebec..."

"...Queensland..."

"I have Qatar, and don't tell me you've never heard of it because I just showed you some stamps from there. Queensland gets five, Quebec ten, Qatar ten. Okay, last one. Name, anyone? Come on, come on, show me what you have!"

"No one has anything, so don't show off, Maya. There's no name that begins with Q."

"Speak for yourself, stupid, I have something!"

"Yes dear Mu-mu, what is it?"

"Well...I have Queen Elizabeth..."

"Oh god, you must have eaten your pea brain for lunch. *Queen* is not a name. You should get minus hundred points for that! See, Maya, no one has anything."

"Hold on, Hema. Wait till it's my turn, okay? So, we start with Mumtaz, and she has nothing. So we move on to Hema, and she's a blank. Sadhana? Nothing? And Milly? And Bomb-bomb Simi? Nothing at all. What a bore. So it's my turn, hmm?"

"Look Maya you know damn well it's your turn."

"I have *Quetzalcoatl!* Q-U-E-T-Z-A-L-C-O-A-T-L. If you don't believe me—obviously you never believe me—find today's *Indian Express* and there's a story and his name is in there. I get fifty points, everyone else gets zero. You'll never catch up so let's just end the game now, okay? Everyone can take a fifteen point lead next time."

Mrs. DeSouza slapped the table with every beat.

"*Three* plus *six* plus *nine* minus *two* divide by *four* minus *two* divide by *two*. Give-me-the-answer-*YOU!*"

DeSouza kept thumping on the table in the dead silence of the classroom. It was like listening to a funeral drum. Long after she screamed *YOU!* she would still be deciding which girl to call on. Finally she would spot her victim and use her chin to point. She never looked at me, because then I would give her the answer. DeSouza didn't like correct answers.

"How you brainless people made it to the fourth, god only knows." DeSouza stuck her chin out and threw the chalk from her hand to the back of the room. Of course, it hit Savitri.

"Come here, you! Always sitting in the back and doing nothing for good. You people need a good slap to wake up." DeSouza threw another piece of chalk at the girl. Poor Savitri. She picked up the chalk and came to the front. DeSouza slapped her hard, then rubbed her chalky fingers onto Savitri's face.

"Dirty girl," DeSouza hissed through her teeth. "Doesn't bathe. Look at her ugly dark skin. I'll fix it!" DeSouza stood back. Savitri's face was covered with white powder. DeSouza grabbed her shoulder and pushed her to the blackboard.

"Are you deaf? I want the answer!"

Savitri wrote 1 in a small hand. Poor Savitri. Mrs. DeSouza didn't like correct answers.

"Oh, so you are feeling brainy today? Let's see if you are more clever. Write the thirteen times table. Quickly now."

Savitri positioned the chalk firmly between her thumb and forefinger, and DeSouza slapped her hand so the chalk fell to the floor.

"Don't they speak English in your house? I said *quickly!*"

We had to make up our own sum, at least three lines long. I looked over at Milly's paper. It was covered with ink smudges. Her sum was not three lines long.

$12 + 12 + 6 \times 4 - 20 \div 4 - 11 \div 2 + 21 \times 2 + 4 \times 3 + 20 \div 5 \div 4 \times 10 \times 10 - 200 \div 40 - 20 = \underline{\quad}$

"How silly to have your sum end in zero!" I whispered. "Zero,

zero, nice and round, nothing lost and nothing found!" I covered my mouth and snorted.

"It doesn't end in zero," she hissed back angrily. "It ends in *one!*"

I laughed aloud. The entire class must have heard me, but DeSouza wouldn't look at me. Savitri was slowly writing out 13 x 4 = 52. I wrote on my palm:

> When Mrs. DeSouza was young
> She totally bit off her tongue
> Her mother was frightened
> But dad got enlightened
> And stuffed up her mouth with dung

DeSouza slapped Savitri's hand again, and the chalk fell out. She was just writing 13 x 10 = 130.

I whispered to Milly, "I think DeSouza has a crush on Savi. Always touching her for any small thing."

B.A. wanted to play any game that I liked. I told her she must learn proper English, so it would be like playing with one of my classmates.

"Now you stop this jungleefying like the dirty goonda children or your mummy will come home bhagwanofying like it's the end of the world!"

B.A. was my special name for Ba, my mother's mother, who could as easily have been my father's mother, for all the resemblance the two women bore to each other. Like magnets, all three generations repelled at opposite poles, so that my grandmother and I, who were outside my mother's magnetic force field, were stuck on each other.

Everyone said that B.A. and I were completely alike, but we couldn't tell. We stood in front of the mirror to look, but then B.A.

would start telling me about how she got *this* gray hair and when she got *that* wrinkle. I told her that we had to stick together, and she agreed. She really *wanted* to learn English, so I made up a game for her. In the game, I asked her riddles and joke-questions. Earlier, I'd written down all the answers and put them in the Lucky Dip jar. If she couldn't guess the answer she had to pay one rupee for one chance at Lucky Dip—to scoop out the correct answer. Sometimes it took a lot of dips.

We kept a notebook of the riddles, and that was helping B.A. with her English. "Crackpotted," she mumbled angrily while floating her teeth in the sink. "Kung Fu said, Man standing on toilet gets a crackpot."

"No, no!" I laughed. "That's not right. It's…Confucius say, Man standing on toilet get high on pot. Try this one. Why did the chicken cross the road?" I asked.

"What, our own Nepean Sea Road?" she asked in turn.

We kept a notebook of Playboy's Party Jokes.

"Minimum. A small British mother." I giggled as I wrote it down.

"Yes, yes, *Nanima*. Heh-heh-heh," B.A. snorted happily.

We worked on card games. Rummy, gin rummy, golden rummy, 2-3-5, seven hands, whist, canasta, wild eights, crazy eights, Uno, hearts, queen of spades, Oklahoma, patience, solitaire, spit, mongoose, Jericho. We were on bridge.

"The thing about some games," I told B.A., "is that you can only play if you have good manners."

Mummy's bridge club waited at the table, hungrily eyeing the two-tiered cucumber and butter sandwiches stacked under a damp cloth. Mummy's sing-song floated down the stairs: "Be there in a minute! The stupid ayah is going to catch hell for this."

The bridge parties really wore the ayah out, as she ran between heating the water for Mummy's bath, making the sandwiches, squeezing the lemons to make three pitchers of lemonade, ironing all the saris Mummy couldn't decide between, cutting the imported cheese into cubes and skewering them three at a time with tooth-picks, arranging Mummy's hair into an immaculate bun...

I don't like bridge. It just doesn't have the zing of seven hands or the cunning of mongoose. What good is a game if you have to be half-dead to play it?

The bridge club would finish nibbling on their sandwiches, and at the same time, they would stop smiling. As the cards were dealt, the ladies were just barely breathing, their legs tightly crossed, faces expressionless.

At least in mongoose you could throw your card down, scream, "Mongoose! Mongoose!" at the top of your voice, and the ayah would come running to watch.

If only the ayah spoke some English, the three of us could have had a wonderful time. But B.A. said it was useless to try and teach the ayah anything. She was a servant. What could she learn?

Variations. "Why did the road and the chicken cross?" I asked B.A. hopefully.

B.A. nodded enthusiastically and I ran to throw the answer into the Lucky Dip jar. Later, B.A. spent twenty rupees trying to find the answer. She was thrilled that it was taking her so long. She wanted to go on all night. But finally the ayah came by and plucked the answer right out. Her fingers smelled of garlic and coconut, and B.A. crumpled the answer and threw it away without looking at it.

"Did you hear about the Italian who died drinking milk?"

The joke book was very funny upside down and everyone was already giggling.

"I know what! When DeSouza comes in today, Savitri should

read her sum like this: 'One plus one cow plus one Italian'...wait, wait! And then, 'the answer is...' and Mu-Mu should say something really funny like 'But Queen Elizabeth is a name!' and I bet DeSouza will give all of us ten out of ten for making her laugh."

"I give up. What's the answer."

"Wait, wait, tell it again."

"Did you hear about the Italian who died drinking milk? Come on now, or I'll put the book away." I lifted the lid of my desk.

"Okay, okay. What's this book anyway? Where did you get it? Next time when DeSouza wants something to throw, just say, 'Oh Miss! Why waste good school chalk, try this lovely foreign book instead.'"

"Let her finish! I give up."

"The cow sat on him."

"One cow divided into one Italian..."

"Wait a sec...what?"

"Are you deaf? You want Maya to repeat everything! Didn't you hear about the Italian? He died drinking milk. What's so great about that. Foreigners are funny people, drinking milk when they're so old."

"I have a baby brother. I can drink milk whenever I want."

"What, your own mother's milk?! Poor woman, have pity on her. Her boobs will droop to the floor."

"Did you hear about the Polish submarine?" I opened up my upside down book and tried to find the right page.

"What's Polish?"

"Same as Italian, stupid. What's the answer? I give up."

"Wait. I can't find it." I thumbed through the marked jokes. How many Polacks...Polish beauty pageant...Polish national dish...

"I can't find it. Something about sinking..."

"Eh, Maya! Didn't you bring the cards?"

I had told them I would teach them a game played with six packs of cards.

"Join all the desks at the corners, otherwise the cards will fall in between the cracks."

"But what are we playing?"

"Just fix the tables first! Where's Bomb-bomb Simi? Isn't she playing?"

"She went home for lunch."

"I have six packs. Somebody else has to join in."

"All the other girls are playing hoppers and skippers downstairs, fourth standard against the sixth. No chance anyone will come up."

"Wait a sec…did Savitri come today? Let me go find her. Shuffle each pack properly, then each of you take one. I'll be right back."

I looked down into the courtyard but didn't see Savitri running around. She never played with the others. She wasn't anywhere in the corridors. Maybe DeSouza had taken her into the staff room again to slap her in front of the teachers during lunch. I wasn't allowed in there.

I heard a toilet flush in the bathroom, so I opened the door and went in. Savitri was washing her hands under the tap.

"Want to play in my game?"

She didn't look at me as she turned off the water. There was no towel on which to wipe her hands, so she rubbed them on the hem of her uniform.

"Eh Savitri, do you want to play?"

"No, I don't want to." She walked by me and pushed open the bathroom door. Her eyes were swollen from crying, but her face was calm.

"Look, at least come and watch. It's only cards." I took her by the wrist and pulled her into the classroom.

"Just sit over here and you can join in later." I pointed to the desk next to mine. Savitri sat down without a word and lay her head down on the desk top.

"Okay, everybody got one pack? This game is called 'bluff.' You get rid of all your cards and that's how you win. Arrange the pack in your hand, and when it's your turn, you have to say something like 'three sevens' and put your three cards face down so that we can't see them, like this, and then the next person will say 'two kings' and put two cards down, and then the next person will say 'three aces' and put three cards down, and if it looks like you are lying, then someone can say, 'I call your bluff!' and if you lied and there aren't three aces there, then you have to pick up *all* the cards and put them in your hand, and if you told the truth then the girl who challenged you has to pick up all the cards."

"I can't hold so many cards in my hand!"

"So stuff them down your uniform, stupid!"

"Shut up all of you. Savitri, are you going to play or not?" I shook her arm and held out a pack of cards. Savitri raised her head and looked blankly at me. Her swollen eyes made her look like an old woman. I crammed the cards into her hand and fanned them out a little.

"Now you're in the game. Now you have to be a sport and play." Savitri looked at the cards in her hand, then rubbed her eyes.

"Eh Maya, I know what. Tell us one of your famous jokes. Savitri hasn't heard any of them."

"Not now. Just play."

"Hey Mu-mu, ask Savitri why she never plays catch."

"What do you mean?"

"Milly, will you please *shut up?* Nobody's playing catch right now. Just put your cards down."

"Not only catch, she can't run relay races either, because you have to touch the person, no? The principal said that no one must touch her, and it's Savi's duty to make sure."

"But it's not her fault if someone touches her in catch. It's part of the game."

"Has anybody told DeSouza this? How will that nutcase entertain herself if she can't slap Savi once a day?"

"But look, if you touch her, like this...nothing happens."

"Stop it! You're such shameless creatures, talking about her like she's not here."

"What if the bad luck only happens afterwards? Call me a coward, but I'm not playing! Better to just leave her alone."

"Camel...camel must be neuter, I think. It doesn't look like a he or a she."

"Hmm. We must ride the zoo camel and find out."

B.A. and I were making lists of nouns in English. She liked them all to be masculine, feminine or neuter. The ayah was folding clothes and scratching her legs. She lifted up her sari and showed me the red marks. The mattress she unrolled to sleep on every night had bedbugs.

"Candle. Candle must be masculine because there is a joke about why is a man like a candle."

"Hmm. Which is the answer?"

"Wait, wait, first bring one rupee for Lucky Dip." B.A. shook her head and yawned. "Today I am very poor."

"What does Savitri mean?"

B.A. looked surprised. "That's a funny riddle," she exclaimed.

"No, no, it's not a joke. I'm asking a serious question."

"Savitri was being very faithful. She was getting a prince and was sticking to him even if she was getting killed."

B.A. pulled out a poster of animals and started cutting out the elephant, working carefully to get the skinny tail.

"Was she killed?"

"No, no. She was getting heartache and dying."

"Heart attack?"

"How should I know! Where's the gum bottle?"

"It's near your foot. Which prince did she like?"

"Why you want to know? Is your name changing? You are having your own prince. Don't be taking the other men. This Savitri of course goes with Satyavan. I am Parvati, so I am liking Shiva. Your mummy, she is for Ram, because we are calling her Sita."

"Uh-huh, but who is for me?" The elephant was swimming on the page in a pool of extra glue.

Mummy knocked on the open door, tugging on the hem of her sari. "What are you two up to? Maya, come and help me with my jewelry."

I put down the notebook and stood up. The ayah was about to scratch herself. I pinched her arm as I left the room.

"Which one do you want me to wear?" Mummy was in a good mood, smiling at me through the dressing table mirror. I looked at her sari. Bright orange chiffon with white and yellow flowers. I searched for her blue aquamarine set in the jewelry box.

"Is my bun okay? I did it myself today because I never know whether that stupid ayah washes herself."

"It's fine. What time are you coming back?" I placed the string of aquamarines around her neck and handed her the matching earrings.

"I don't know, sweetie. Ask the cook for your dinner, okay? There's chocolate custard for afterwards." I hated chocolate custard, but B.A. liked it because she could take her teeth out and suck the cooling custard right out of the bowl.

"Mummy, can my friend sleep here one night?"

"What friend? Maya, you don't *have* any friends, remember? Just yesterday Mumtaz's mother was telling me that you're quite a little bully. Don't forget that you're growing up into a young lady and that you need to have lots of nice friends so people don't think there's something wrong with you."

She peered into the mirror, craning her head this way and that, then removed the aquamarine jewelry.

"This blue doesn't match. I don't like blue. I don't wear blue. Only your grandmother likes blue. And speaking of her, how will your Ba feel if you have a friend spending the night? She'll get lonely and her feelings will be hurt."

"B.A. won't mind. All three of us will play together. Mummy, why don't you come and play Lucky Dip with us? It's only fifty paise for one turn if you play, and if you get the right answer, I'll give you all your money back."

"No, no, you and Ba have your fun. Two is company, three's a crowd. Anyway, I'm too old for these silly games, and plus my nail polish is wet and will stick to everything."

"Please? *Please?*"

"No! I don't have time. Why must you ask me to do impossible things at the last minute?"

"Can my friend come over tomorrow night?"

"Yes, yes, yes! Whatever you want. But don't get in a fight with Ba because I won't be here to sort things out. Now let me get dressed in peace. Go!"

"Just wait and see!" Billy Goat was shouting. "You'll end up like those hijras under the bridge!"

Savitri stood in the corridor with no shoes on. Billy Goat had just thrown them away because they were never properly polished.

The lunch bell rang and the girls quickly put away their books and ran down to play in the courtyard. Billy Goat collected her papers with shaking hands and marched out of the class with her nose in the air. Her three long billy goat hairs stuck out stiffly from her chin. As soon as she disappeared down the stairs, I motioned Savitri to come back in.

"I'm staying inside today. Do you want my shoes to go down and play?"

Savitri slowly looked down at her feet, then back up. She shook her head.

"The girls are all stupid. I don't like them."

"Our group is not so stupid. Do you want to play with us?"

"You're all the same. I don't like to play your games. I'm not like you."

Savitri's eyes were red and swollen as usual. Anyone could tell it was from crying, but none of us ever *saw* Savitri cry.

"Everyone has to have some friends."

"I have lots of friends. Where I live. Real big people, grownups. Not sissies like you."

"Hey Maya, do you have a crush on Savi or what? Pestering her all the time."

"Shut your trap, Hema. Nobody asked you."

Savitri made a move to leave the classroom but I grabbed her hand.

"Did you bring any lunch? You can have mine. They're really good jam and butter rolls."

"Look at Maya pushing her pathetic lunch onto Savi like she's a mongrel from the road."

Savitri shook her head. "I don't like sweets. Do you have any chilies to eat?"

Chilies! This girl was mad.

"Sorry, I don't have chilies. But I have some money. Let's go to the Irani restaurant."

"Maya, don't take her! You're not allowed. If the principal sees you, she'll punish you."

"So let her. Come on, let's go."

It was a school rule that students were not allowed to buy food at the restaurant by the school gates. The principal said she was afraid the students would get sick. But when you looked in the restaurant, it was clean and tidy, and the owner was a big Irani woman who was always busy dusting and wiping the tables and counters. The only problem was that sometimes the hijras from under the bridge ate there, and even the teachers were afraid of them, all dressed up in their saris and gaudy makeup.

The schoolgirls referred to the restaurant owner as "Mrs. Irani." She delighted in sneaking a snack to a student pretending to be strolling down the street. The girl would lean back by the side of the entrance, and a quick exchange of money and packaged snack would take place behind the girl's back. The snack was stuffed into the pocket of the uniform and the girl went on her way.

I pulled Savitri into the restaurant and we sat at a table. The restaurant was empty. Mrs. Irani came rushing over, peering anxiously out into the street to see if we had been spotted.

"We want something with chilies," I ordered. "And she wants a cup of tea."

Mrs. Irani raised her eyebrows in amusement. "I'll bring you chicken patties," she said.

Savitri's face softened, and she smiled. "I love chicken patties," she sighed.

"I'll tell the cook at home and bring them for lunch tomorrow. You can share."

Savitri was surprised. "You're Muslim? You cook meat in your house?"

"No. But the cook gets some from the Christian people next door. The ayah there is always making eyes at our cook. Are you Muslim?"

Savitri laughed. "Where I live, you don't have to be Muslim or Christian or anything special to eat meat. I have friends who give me some."

"The same friends who give you chilies?"

"Yes. All the men have a competition to see who can eat the most chilies. Sometimes I win."

"Which men?"

Mrs. Irani arrived with the steaming patties, and Savitri snatched one off the plate and stuffed it in her mouth, chewing rapidly. She shielded her mouth with one hand as she ate.

I took a bite. The patty was full of green chili, which made me cough. I walked to the icebox to get a cold drink. When I returned to the table, all the patties were gone and Savitri was slurping noisily on her tea.

"Why do you let DeSouza beat you all the time? Doesn't it hurt you?"

Savitri looked up quickly, frowning.

"If it hurts you, wouldn't it hurt me?" she asked, annoyed.

I shrugged. "I don't know. People are different. If a teacher hit me that much, every day, I would complain to my parents. Why don't you?"

Savitri kept her eyes on the tea.

"Maybe you're right," she said evenly. "Maybe it doesn't hurt."

Mrs. Irani brought the bill on a small metal plate and sat down at the table. She was a large woman, and wore a shapeless dress that looked like a housecoat.

"You know," said Mrs. Irani, "this girl looks very familiar to me." She pointed at Savitri, who ignored her. I pulled some money out of my pocket. Mrs. Irani reached forward and firmly tilted up Savitri's chin.

"Ah!" She exclaimed. "Now I remember. I see you and your mother getting off the bus every morning in front of my house." She turned to me. "I live two streets away, you see, and the same bus that stops outside the school here first stops right outside my house. Sometimes I see this one and her mother get off outside my house, and I know from her uniform that she goes to this school. Every morning I wonder, But why don't they just get off the bus in front of the school? Why unnecessarily walk all the way from here? Always the mother walks far in front, while this rascal girl stays behind."

The big woman stood up slowly and cracked her knuckles.

"I also have a daughter your age," she sighed. "But where do I have the money to put her in a fancy school? At least if I were a teacher, like this one's mother," she nodded at Savitri, "then my girl could also come to the school for free."

I was shocked. Savitri's mother a teacher? Which one? I stared at Savitri, my mind racing. I matched her face with all the teachers in the school. Small face, dark skin, sulky expression...Oh god! It couldn't be.

Savitri stood up, annoyed.

"Don't listen to her. She's lying. I don't *have* a mother."

"Come *on!*" I shouted, pulling Savitri by the hand. "The car is this way."

"No, no, no!" Savitri gasped and struggled. "I can't go. I don't want to go. I have so much work to do!"

I knew that if I asked Savitri beforehand about spending the night at my house, she would never agree. So I waited until the last bell rang and the whole schoolful of girls raced down the corridors to get out of that building as quickly as possible. In that mad rush, I clung to Savitri and steered her out of the gate. Outside, when she realized that I was serious, she started twisting and turning in a panic to get free of me.

Finally my driver spotted me in the crowd and came running over to help me.

"Hold her, hold her!" I screamed. "She has to come home with us."

The driver and I dragged Savitri to the car and bundled her into the front seat. The driver and I got in on either side of her so she was wedged between us. She slumped back against the seat and kicked the dashboard in anger. We locked our doors. The driver was laughing, thinking it was all a game. He quickly started the car and we drove off.

We passed Billy Goat, pushing her way through the crowds of vegetable vendors and shoppers on the pavement.

"Hey, Savi, guess what. I made up a limerick about Billy Goat. Want to hear it?

> Billy Goat was walking to school
> Her brain overflowing with drool
> She tripped on a stone
> And broke every bone
> And just died there, bloody old fool."

Savitri stopped kicking the dashboard and snorted with pleasure.

"That's really funny," she said. "It's just like a real poem."

The driver was still excited, beaming from ear to ear.

"Maya-baby friend?" he asked happily. "New friend? Good! Very good."

"Do you really *have* any friends?" I asked Savitri.

"Do you?" Savitri shot back.

"I'm only asking! You don't have to get so angry."

"Do I ask you questions all the time? How would *you* feel?"

"You are so funny," I exclaimed. "First you don't talk for donkeys years, then when you finally say something, you start fighting!"

"So stop being so nosey. It's none of your business anyway. Just because I go to this stupid school, you think you know everything about me. But I'm not like you stupid rich people."

The driver kept looking at us and grinning madly.

"New friend! Good. *Very* good."

B.A. looked at Savitri in disgust. Savitri sat hunched over on the bed, looking like she was ready to sprint out of the room.

"This is your friend? But she's just a *chhaprasi!* A sweeper's daughter."

"She is not!" I shouted. "She's a Christian, like the people next door. She's my friend from school."

"Stupid girl, these Christians were all untouchable chhaprasis before. That's why they became Christians. But underneath they're still same-same! My god. And here I am thinking your mother is sending you to school for girls of good background. Where is she? Give me her number, I will call at once."

The ayah entered the room, saw Savitri scowling on the bed and stopped dead in her tracks.

"Oh bhagwan!" She looked frightened. She walked up to Savitri, who glared at her. The ayah spoke to Savitri in Konkani, the coastal dialect from the region south of Bombay.

"You're not my daughter?" asked the ayah.

"Of course not!" Savitri snapped back in Konkani.

"You look like my daughter!" whimpered the ayah, and she started bawling, wiping her eyes with the end of her sari.

"She has a daughter?" I whispered to B.A. "Did you know that?"

"Of course I don't!" B.A. was furious. "What do I care if this servant is pulling out *pigs* from between her legs!"

"I haven't seen my daughter in so long," cried the ayah. "She's growing up and soon I'll have to send her away. I want her to come here now and be with me."

The ayah squatted down on the floor and hugged her knees. She was very sad. I sat down next to her.

"We'll ask Mummy," I offered, hesitant. "I'm sure she'll say it's okay. She always needs more help in the house."

"We'll ask *Mummy*," Savitri repeated in a mocking voice. "No *Mummy* cares about other people's children."

"Don't talk like that!" I cried, stung by Savitri's cruel words. "Just because *your* mummy doesn't care. Worse than that, DeSouza is afraid of me. *Me!* A ten-year-old girl she doesn't even know."

Savitri narrowed her eyes and spat, "Don't keep calling her my mother. And she's not half as afraid of you as she is of me. She knows that I'm going to kill her one day. Everyone knows. They're all just waiting for it to happen."

Savitri chewed on her fingernails furiously, lost in thought. I was suddenly afraid, and stepped back and took B.A.'s hand. This girl was very strange.

"But if you're going to kill her, why do you let her beat you?"

Savitri rubbed her swollen eyes and yawned.

"It's the only time she can find me. She knows I won't run away from school."

"What do you mean? Don't you go home after school?"

Savitri grimaced and waved away the idea.

"Of course not. Why should I? I go to play with my friends."

B.A. nudged me in irritation.

"Why don't you just give her some money for the bus and send her home? You must understand, she is a junglee girl. She is not one of us."

"No! Maya-baby, no!" The ayah came waddling across the bedroom floor and gripped my arm. "For the sake of a poor old woman, let her stay the night. Only this one night. Let me be with my daughter just this once. I am begging!" She pressed her palms together, pleading.

B.A. and I looked at each other. B.A. was angry. I squeezed her fingers and put my arm around her in a hug.

"We'll have lots of fun. We'll all play together, I promise. You can play Lucky Dip for free, as many times as you want. Okay?"

B.A. sighed loudly a few times, then turned away.

"My pressure is going up!" she groaned. "You're all killing me, I know it." She left the room.

Savitri stood up and stretched. Under the white pinafore, her body was all bones.

"Don't you at least want to call your mother?" I asked Savitri.

She looked at me as though I were crazy.

"Call? We don't have a phone! We live in a slum. I usually stay out all night. Today is Friday. She won't even think about me until Monday morning when it's time to go to school."

Savitri walked toward me, and I stepped back. She could see that I was scared.

"You want to have some fun, no? You said you wanted to play with me."

I nodded.

"Good," said Savitri. "I'll teach you some games that you can also play with boys. With *men*. Then you don't have to play with those stupid girls in school. You just shut up that granny of yours and we'll have lots of fun."

I'm looking at them, at the two of them. They are finally asleep. She is as small as a baby in the arms of the other. In the arms of her mother. They are locked together, leg over leg, arm over arm, like a human puzzle.

They laughed and joked in Konkani all evening. I couldn't understand everything. She said to me, making fun of me, This is my mother. See? See how much she loves me, how she wants to be with me. Not like the other one. This is my mother.

What is her real daughter's name? I asked Savitri.

Same as hers, she replied.

Same as hers? I didn't know she had a name. We call her ayah.

If you have a name why wouldn't she also? You rich people are really senseless. It's time for you to learn something useful now. I'll teach you that game I was telling you. It's the same thing your parents do at nighttime. Do you know what your parents do?

Go to parties? I guessed. Every night.

Savitri laughed. She thought it was very funny. She told the ayah in Konkani what she had asked me and what I had said. The ayah got angry. The two of them started fighting. The ayah pulled Savitri out of the room. They kept arguing.

Finally Savitri came back into the room and jumped on the bed. Too bad, she cried, jumping up and down. The ayah doesn't want me to teach you the game. She thinks it's bad for you or something.

I was still scared of her.

The ayah combed and oiled Savitri's hair. Then she gave Savitri a wash, pouring tumbler after tumbler of hot water down her back.

B.A. and I ate quietly at the dinner table, while the ayah sat with Savitri in the servants' room, feeding her bite after bite of chicken patties. They were laughing like madwomen.

Finally, they fell asleep on the ayah's thin bedroll on the floor by my bed. The guest bed next to mine remained empty. I watched them to see if they were pulling another joke on me, just pretending in each other's arms. But they were stuck to each other. These two had a real boy-girl crush on each other.

After watching them for a long time I finally fell asleep.

"Maya!" Mummy was shouting in my ear. "Wake up for god's sake."

I opened my eyes, and there she was, with tears running down her face. "Are you all right? Did she hurt you? Your Ba is so upset. She told us first thing when we walked in that some low-class girl forced you to bring her home and play with her."

It was early in the morning, before sunrise. I sat up in bed and wiped my eyes.

"And look!" my mother cried. "She's torn up every single answer from your Lucky Dip jar! Oh my poor baby, you must feel terrible!"

Mummy pulled me to her and sniffled a little. I peered over her shoulder at the shreds of paper sprinkled over the bed next to mine. On the floor, the Lucky Dip jar stood empty.

"And Ba said that this wretched girl is in your school! That is the part I just don't understand. We can't have you mixing with low-class good-for-nothings."

Mummy wiped away her tears.

"I just can't believe that the principal has allowed this to happen. She knows how much money we donate to the school every year. She should have known better than to let this happen. I have no choice but to pull you out of that school."

"What?" I screamed. "But I don't want to leave. I like it there!"

"Your poor Ba, you should see her. She's absolutely heartbroken. She says that no matter how hard she tried, she couldn't influence you. She is on an indefinite fast and has taken a vow of silence. She says she will pray for you. She won't talk to any of us until she sees you settled in a new school. She said, No more English school. Put her in a proper Gujarati school, where they won't fill her brain with all kinds of funny ideas."

"But I like it there!" I repeated, bewildered by all the information. Overnight, B.A. had turned into a nutcase!

"That girl, she lives in a slum! Can you imagine? She's filthy, full of disease and god knows what else. She stole all your Ba's Lucky Dip money and tore up all the answers. The news might even be worse than that, but your Ba has stopped talking to us." Mummy closed her eyes and shivered.

"I blame myself for not being here to protect you. I promise I'll stay home every night from now on, my darling Maya."

"But she didn't do anything! She's just different, she's not afraid like all the others."

"I blame myself, sweetie. All this time, stuck with only the dirty ayah and Ba, you must have been missing your own mother so much! I'll talk to your daddy. I'm sure he'll understand. From now on, every night, you can sleep with us."

"In the nighttime?"

"Yes, my darling, in the nighttime, when the whole world is crawling with spirits and ghosts, your mummy will keep you safe."

"Maya, I swear, you are *so* lucky to be getting out of this stinking school! I wish I had your mother."

"The principal is shitting in her pants, you know. No Maya, no money."

"But the one good thing, at least, is that finally DeSouza is going. Hopefully to the nuthouse. And that sourpuss Savitri is also leaving. Did you know she was taking drugs? Brown sugar or something. Good riddance!"

"You know what I heard? DeSouza lives in a slum! Can you believe it? A Maths teacher living in the slums! She has no shame, teaching in a private school."

"Hey but now that Maya is going, no more jokes, or card games or anything. We'll be forced to go down and play running games."

"Might as well learn to run now, stupid. One of these days you'll be running after children, and then your legs will really have to move. I can just see it! Mu-mu, running around the house with her boobs down to *here!*"

"Shut up, for god's sake, all of you. I'm leaving in a few days. I don't need to hear this idiotic babble of yours." I pulled out a single pack of cards and started dealing them out for solitaire. "We should all take a hint from my grandmother and take a vow of silence. Life is much better that way."

The group of girls stared at me unbelievingly. Vow of silence? I looked at them with a serious expression. They appeared so shocked that I burst into laughter. I put away the cards and motioned them all forward into a huddle.

"All right," I whispered. "One last game for you before I leave this school. It's called Lucky Dip. You've all played it before, right? At the fair, you can play Lucky Dip for one rupee. You stick your hand into the bin and pull out the piece of paper, and whatever prize is written on the paper, that's the prize you win, correct?"

The girls nodded in unison. The light shone in their eyes.

"In this version, the only thing different is that the prize you win is not some stupid plastic toy, it's actually a prize that you *lose*. That you want to get rid of. Okay? So, you put the name of each teacher in the school on one piece of paper. Then you put all the names in a jar. Got that?"

"Maya...I think you're just making this all up as you go."

"Ya, who ever heard of teachers being part of a game?"

"And anyway who's got rupees in their pocket to play Lucky Dip? Just 'cause your parents have all the money."

"I'd rather run up and down the stairs five times than learn any more of your funny games, Maya."

"Shut up and listen, you nincompoops! There isn't much time."

I paused and took a deep breath. I winked at the group.

"In the afternoon break, pull one name out of the jar, run down to the bridge and tell the hijras that today is the birthday of Mrs. X, say, Billy Goat. Tell the hijras that it is a custom in our school for the teacher to give everyone a present who wishes her "Happy Birthday." They should wait until she comes out of the school, then surround her and clap and laugh and sing "Happy Birthday" until she gives them some money. Got it? The point is that the teachers are all dead scared of the hijras, and would never give them money. So tell them they should follow the teacher home if they have to, because it just means that she is shy."

The girls were dumbfounded. They couldn't believe it.

"They'll...they'll just *die*. The teachers are really frightened of them."

"The old grannies like Billy Goat will have a heart attack! Right there outside the gate."

"And the principal! Just imagine. With that iron face of hers. She'll run screaming for help!"

"And...and...maybe if we arrange it every day, each teacher one by one, then the whole school will close down and *nobody* will have to study here!"

"Maya! You're a bloody genius. The whole school will shut down."

"Let's try this Lucky Dip. A going away present for Maya."

I sat back and smiled to myself. They were going to try it. They looked determined. They might just pull it off.

"But that's not all," I said sharply.

They looked at me with the same old light in their eyes, the group of girls who stayed upstairs in the lunch break.

"This is for Savi," I reminded them solemnly. "A going away present for Savi. This game is our special present to her."

"God, Maya! Don't tell me you still have a crush on that mad girl. You shouldn't mix with those slum types. They don't know anything about being ladylike."

"Shut up, Milly. What's it to you if they had a crush on each other? Everyone has to have a friend sometime. Otherwise people will think you're strange."

The Cure

It all started when I began to grow. My mother watched me closely. Very closely. She couldn't believe I was destined to be a giant. Every day the tile around my room door was scratched with heel marks. Every night the keyhole to my room was smeared with lipstick.

I didn't mind my mother breathing heavily outside the room. I felt sorry for her, so I let her watch. I spent a lot of time sitting at my desk. I marked how my legs had grown to such a length that my knees scraped painfully against the underside of the desk. I clearly remembered my legs dangling high off the ground at that same desk. I would lean forward over the table and lay my arms out in front of me on the big pink blotter. My fingers touched the wall behind the desk with ease. I remembered when I had to pull my body over the table up to my stomach in order to touch the wall behind the desk. I liked to sit there at my old desk and imagine how small my body had once been.

I also spent time looking at myself. I now had to stand far back to see my full frame in the cupboard mirror. My face was no longer in line with the top of the mirror when I stood flush against it. I could no longer lean against the cool surface and see my twin face joined wherever I desired, at the cheek or at the nose or at the tip of my tongue.

My mother blamed herself for allowing me to wear her heels when I was younger. She was convinced that my height signaled that I was meant to be a boy. Her ill luck at having produced a daughter meant she would suffer in her next birth. "At least you didn't turn out a *blackie* on top of it," she muttered in consolation.

My parents nervously watched me grow and grow, until I was so tall that my father was embarrassed to stand next to me in public. My father stopped speaking to my mother as he no longer believed that I was his child. He also felt that no man in his right mind would marry a giantess like myself and resigned himself to the fact that I would remain an unmarried dependent for life.

Every day my mother recounted to me sadly how much she used to love me, and how she wished she loved me still. Until the age of eleven, I was the apple of my mother's eye. I was also a carbon copy of her. She was small and fair, with large eyes and a perfectly straight nose. At the age of eleven I began to grow, and my small fair body became a looming tower that stooped forward over everyone. My limbs were long and thin, but my mother said I was obviously eating too much. She cut out sweets, snacks and soft drinks from my diet. She fed me milk of magnesia every night, to help "flush out the excess body matter."

For two years my height increased at a steady pace. There seemed to be no end in sight. She asked all her friends what to do about her "jumbo child." The women suggested ice packs to shrink the flesh, and gas-forming foods to keep my long frame bent over double. They wanted mother to take me on a pilgrimage, because I was obviously *too proud*, standing tall over all men, my elders, the gods and all. Mrs. Mishra suggested sending me to a doctor. Why not? These days doctors have a cure for everything.

The driver Ramdass was my constant companion. He didn't care that I was too tall, in fact it had never even entered his consciousness. To him, I was still "Baby," still the young child of his employer. Even though he was on "house duty," Ramdass referred to himself proudly as "Ramdass, office driver." He had a crew cut of gray hair and sweat stains in the armpits of his starched uniform which he wore unbuttoned in the Bombay heat.

In the evenings, after picking me up from school, Ramdass was at my disposal. We could take a drive anywhere we wanted to. Every evening without fail, I would heave my schoolbag onto the front seat, climb into the back and stretch my legs out along the seat.

"Worli, *direct!*" I would announce to Ramdass, and he would speed through the crowds of school girls, hawkers, laborers and office workers to get me to Worli Sea Face. How diligently he coaxed the big blue Ambassador, elegantly turning the wheel with sometimes languid, sometimes rapid gestures while dancing from the knees down as he alternated pressing the foot pedals. He swayed from side to side, his body completely absorbed into the motion of the car. Ramdass would watch the traffic and I would watch Ramdass. His front-seat ballet would make me drowsy and

I would lie back with eyes half-closed.

Eventually we would turn off the main road onto the wide sweeping curve of the Sea Face road. Ramdass would break into a smile as he shifted gears and raced the car down the usually empty road. The breeze would whip up my hair like a shredded black flag. At the end of the sea wall, Ramdass would pull to the side and park. He and I would step out of the car and walk toward the raised sea wall. It was a few feet off the sidewalk. I would walk quickly along the narrow wall, swaying from side to side to keep my balance. Ramdass would march alongside with one hand ready to grasp me in case I lost my balance. The waves would glide in to the bottom of the wall, breaking softly without spraying me. In this way we would walk the length of the wall, first in the direction away from the car, and then back towards it.

Every evening as dusk settled onto the city, we returned to where the car was parked and waiting for us was the man we called the *Suitwallah*. He was always there for our return, seated on that sea wall as though he had been sitting forever. We never saw him coming.

The Suitwallah had a long thin face and long thin hands. He always wore a three-piece suit. He looked like a schoolmaster. He sat facing me with his hands placed on his thighs. He would watch me without a word, until I finally broke his gaze by walking past him. Then he would nod at Ramdass, who would courteously nod back. He never turned his face to follow us as we got into the parked car and drove off. Sometimes I had Ramdass wait a few minutes before turning on the car, just to see whether Suitwallah would turn around to look at the car, but he never did turn around, as though we had disappeared from existence once we stepped around him.

One afternoon, when Ramdass came to pick me up from school, my mother was in the back seat. She watched me glumly as I bent down to half my height in order to climb into the car. She sniffed disdainfully as I sat sideways on the seat to provide my long legs with extra room.

"Lady Doctor!" my mother ordered the back of Ramdass' head. Ramdass looked at me frantically from the corner of his eye, waiting for me to confirm the order. He sensed that something was very wrong. I waved him on.

The lady doctor shrieked as I entered her office. She pulled the spectacles off her nose and stared at me in a rage. She waved her arms about, as if asking the universe to explain my presence. Finally she recovered her voice.

"Oh you poor thing!" she exclaimed and rushed to embrace my mother. My mother's composure crumbled entirely and she began sobbing in the doctor's arms.

"Oh, it must be so hard for you!" the doctor groaned sympathetically, wiping my mother's tears and kissing her on the head while motioning irritatedly for me to take a seat.

My mother wiped her nose with the end of her sari and covered her face with her hands, sobbing like a little girl. The lady doctor steered my mother towards the examining table and helped her onto the padded surface. My mother sat slumped over like a rag doll. The lady doctor paced up and down the room, frowning and gesticulating in silence. Then she stopped in front of me and straightened her stethoscope.

"Fundamentally over-sexed!" hissed the lady doctor, pointing at me. "Danger to society. Sex hormones out of control. Shameless and uninhibited. Look how she tempts!"

The lady doctor marched over to where I sat sprawled in the

armchair, grabbed my thighs and pressed them tightly together until they were sealed shut. She held them that way until I crossed my legs.

She turned back to my mother and grasped her hands, squeezing and releasing them while shaking her head dumbly to and fro. My mother leaned forward with quivering lips as the lady doctor frowned and searched for the right words.

"Just take it, madam," she exhaled at last, "that your suffering in this lifetime will be limitless…"

My mother cried out in shock.

"…unless you take my advice."

The lady doctor marched to her desk and quickly wrote out a prescription. She tore it off the pad, then wrote down some more information on the back. The lady doctor pressed the buzzer on her desk and instantly her office attendant walked in.

"Next!" the lady doctor ordered the attendant, and he nodded and closed the door. Our time was up.

The lady doctor steered my mother outside the office to where Ramdass was parked, and I followed. The doctor pressed the paper into my mother's hand.

"My dear lady, here is a tranquilizer prescription for you. I can see you haven't been getting much sleep." My mother whispered grateful thanks.

"And on the back is the name of a doctor I know." The lady doctor dropped her voice to a whisper. "He is a licensed *sexologist*."

The lady doctor paused, and stiffened her back.

"You will understand everything," she announced haughtily, "when I ask you: 'Can one woman ever really know another?'" She sniffed and looked me up and down.

"This girl needs to be cured by a proper *man*. Dr. Doctor is the one for her."

I bit into the glass of milk until my teeth hurt. Suddenly the glass cracked. The broken piece came away in my mouth and the milk spilled onto the table. My mother looked at me tiredly from across the dining table. The tranquilizers were keeping her groggy all day long.

"Good," she said yawning, "one less thing for you to eat. Anyway, milk is meant for a growing child, not for a demoness."

We were waiting at the dining table for the arrival of Dr. Doctor. The name, he had assured my mother on the phone, was genuine and not to be worried about. His ancestors for generations had been doctors, and doctoring was in his blood.

The bell rang sharply and my mother sat up. Lakshman, the servant, could be heard running quickly from the back of the house, through the kitchen, and out into the reception area to answer the door. After some discussion, the servant stuck his head in the dining room, peevishly snapped, "Doctor sahib," and retired to the kitchen.

Dr. Doctor entered the dining room, and I gasped. He stopped in shock as he recognized me. He dropped his medical bag onto the carpet.

"So we meet at last," he murmured.

Standing in front of me was the Suitwallah from Worli Sea Face. He was even thinner than he appeared while seated. His face was hollow-cheeked with dark slashes for eyes and mouth. His legs were no thicker than bamboo poles and his cadaverous frame stooped forward, as though unable to support his narrow torso. His eyes gleamed and his eyebrows froze into lopsided arches. I was facing him and he marched toward me. My mother's small body was almost entirely hidden in the plush swivel chair and Dr. Doctor spun her around to face him. He stood over her, his thin lips curling with a mix of eagerness and impatience. He stuck out his hand. It was long and pale and hairless.

"At your service, madam," he rumbled in a surprisingly deep voice.

My mother cautiously touched her hand to the doctor's, then swiveled around to face me.

"She's the one," my mother pointed. "Cure her."

Dr. Doctor looked at me and smiled. He already knew me well. What had he thought of me all those hundreds of times he had locked his eyes with mine.

"I am well acquainted with her case," the doctor said pleasantly. "I have been watching her development for years. Certainly a rare specimen."

My mother puzzled over the doctor's statements.

"Excuse me, doctor, but do we know you from somewhere?"

"Your daughter's height is a topic of much discussion in Bombay. We were bound to meet sooner or later. I have already made notes on her case in anticipation of this event."

My mother's face crumpled at the mention of my height.

"Won't you stay for tea?" my mother cried as she rushed to the kitchen shouting "Lakshman! Chai!" to cover up her tears.

Dr. Doctor motioned for me to stand up, then he walked all around me, sighing and clucking his tongue.

"Hunh...," he hummed with wonder, "hmm...now, let's see...uh-huh..."

When my mother returned with the tea, he took a chair next to her.

"Madam, in all my years, I have seen nothing like this. Breathtaking opportunity. Once in a lifetime chance! I would be interested even in taking her on as a charity case."

My mother reached forward fearfully and clutched the doctor's hands. "Please, I insist on paying you *highest* fees. You are a specialist of *great repute*. Find a cure, that's all I ask. Turn her back into my innocent darling."

Dr. Doctor whipped out his calling card and turned it over. He wrote out the time of his next visit.

"You see, madam, it looks like a *grave* imbalance...," the doctor paused, irritated by my mother's ingratiating smiling and nodding.

"This is not to be taken lightly, madam! It is a one-in-a-million imbalance of the...uh...of the...ohhhh...feminine *fluids*, let us say. I must monitor this condition by taking *regular* samples of her female waters. Do you get my meaning? It is a complicated process but you have no cause for alarm because *I* will come to *her*. Best to see such once-in-a-lifetime cases in their own homes, madam, so they feel at ease."

My mother sniffled gratefully and placed a many-folded hundred rupee note in the doctor's palm. He patted my mother's arm and leaned forward intimately.

"I know what it is like having daughters of disposable age, madam. Your pain is mine, madam. I will bring all my knowledge to this case, madam. You can count on me." He collected his doctor's bag and stood up to leave.

"I strongly recommend that you absent yourself for the duration of my weekly visit, madam. Only to make it less *painful* for you, madam, being the girl's mother and all."

I looked at the card he had dropped on the table. Dr. Cyrus Rustom Doctor, M.D., F.R.C.S. Son of Dr. Ardeshir Mehli Doctor, M.D. Grandson of Dr. Kekoo Naoroji Doctor, M.D.

I looked at Dr. Doctor and his face was suddenly stern.

"I will see you next *in your own house*," he warned.

"Don't expect us to meet on *any other path.*" Then he winked, waved his arm in a wide circle and left.

I didn't tell my mother that the doctor and I actually knew each other well. There was no other way to describe our countless daily meetings: my great anticipation at seeing his form slowly materialize as I walked along the sea wall; the long length of time over which we stared at each other without discomfort. I could tell from the way he was accustomed to looking at me that he knew me as a person, not just as a child.

I was curious to see whether I had correctly understood his words as he left the house. I had Ramdass drive me to Worli Sea Face the next day. I walked along the sea wall as usual, but the staring, seated form of the doctor did not appear. He had meant his words. We were now destined to play a different game.

The day before Dr. Doctor was due, I cleaned my room with great excitement. I knew my mother was watching through the keyhole, but I didn't care. The following morning, I rushed down to the car and jumped in breathless next to Ramdass.

"I have a friend coming today!" I sang to him. "Finally, someone to see *me!*"

Ramdass was ecstatic. "A friend for Baby! It is very good. We must buy some sweets to welcome this friend."

Ramdass stopped outside a sweet shop. The shop owner recognized him and waved. Ramdass shouted out an order for a kilo of mixed sweetmeats. When the shop boy came running up with the neatly packaged box, Ramdass paid for it with his own money.

I got home and readied myself for the visit. I tied my hair back, to keep it out of the way. I trimmed my fingernails and toenails, so as to not scratch him accidentally. I brushed my teeth and scraped my tongue clean.

What would the doctor want me to wear? I decided on a dress which could be unbuttoned fully from the collar to the hem, like the gowns in hospitals. When I tried it on, I realized that the hem was higher than the last time I had worn it. My body was continuing to grow.

The house was quiet. My mother was out shopping and our servant Lakshman was out smoking with his friends. The front door was wide open. In my room there was a sealed envelope pinned to my cork board, marked PERSONAL AND CONFIDENTIAL and addressed to Dr. Doctor, M.D. Below the letter, on my desk, I placed the wrapped and ribboned box of sweets.

Dr. Doctor entered the room. He was wearing a brown three-piece suit with a maroon tie. His oiled hair was as black and sticky as shoe polish. He wiped the sweat off his brow and neck and locked his gaze on me. The hair on my arms rose in waves.

"Will you have something to eat?" I asked.

"No, no," he waved like an orchestra conductor. "I have not come to a restaurant. I am here to diagnose the aberrance of your maidenhead, a task that undoubtedly increases my thirst. Water is all I ask."

I went into the kitchen and opened the refrigerator. There I found chilled coconut water in a glass, neatly covered by a lace cloth weighted down on the edges with beads. When I returned to the room, Dr. Doctor was looking through my closet.

"You wear men's clothes?" he asked, pointing to my collection of trousers. I looked at the doctor's trousers. They were drainpipes, narrow in the leg and tight and creased across his hips.

"My pants all button on the *side*," I emphasized.

"Oh-ho!" the doctor chuckled. "So you are indeed a woman." He motioned me towards him, put his hands on my shoulders and turned me in one direction and then the other to see what I was wearing.

"Ah, good," he cried, "you are wearing a dress. This delicate procedure, you see, requires that I...well, that uh....a dress is very good."

The doctor sat at my desk and opened his doctor's bag. His long fingers lazily pushed aside instruments and papers until he found what he wanted. He pulled out two thin glass slides wrapped in tissue paper and lay them gingerly on the desk, flicking away specks of dust. His eye caught sight of the envelope my mother had pinned to the cork board. He held the envelope up to the light, saw that it contained a hundred-rupee note and stuffed it into his coat pocket. He noticed the box of sweets and turned to me in surprise.

"Is it your birthday today?" He quickly unwrapped and opened the box and thrust a sweet into his mouth. "Now come here," he commanded and patted his knee. I walked over to him, wondering if he would feed me a sweet as well. He put his hands on my hips and looked up at me.

"Good, good," he said, squinting at my face. "You are too tall for your eyes to be a distraction." He took the hem of my dress in his hands and tugged on it as he spoke.

"Listen carefully now. I have to perform this procedure, which will take place in the lower half of your body. It might take a few minutes, because you are young and not accustomed to such manner of contact. You don't even know it, but there is a special kind of fluid in you, that I must have to make my diagnosis. At each appointment I will need to test this fluid and I *cannot* stress enough how *important* it is that you simply *learn to relax!*"

Quick as a whip, Dr. Doctor reached under my dress and pulled down my panties. They fell to the ground, and I stepped aside and kicked them away.

"Now bend a little at the knees," he murmured, then steadied his head against my stomach. He placed one hand around the back of my legs and brought the other to his mouth. He licked the index finger front and back, then reached between my legs. His hand was ticklish on my skin. I leaned my arm against the cork board to keep my balance.

"It's like finally meeting a pen pal," I whispered to myself.

"You're such a big girl," the doctor responded, leaning intently against my hip. I could feel his thumb and two fingers pushing against my thighs. The other two fingers were pushing inside me, but I couldn't quite understand where. Was he trying to find my stomach from the inside? His pushing made me sway. He held tighter around my legs to keep me still. His fingers made me more ticklish and I laughed. Deep inside me he had found a pouch of skin! It felt like what the pouch of a kangaroo must be like, only on the inside.

"This will take time," he murmured into my hip.

I couldn't stop laughing. The doctor also smiled.

"When you were ready to be born, the doctor put his fingers inside your mother like this to tickle you and wake you up. That's why you're so ticklish."

I could feel his fingers slowly, gently, going round and round and up and down inside my pouch of skin. The rest of my body seemed to be floating away into the air. I looked down from the ceiling at the sight of the doctor bent over and clasping me, as though asking my forgiveness.

Suddenly the tickle inside became very strong, burning me, and I had to put a hand on the doctor's head to keep from falling. I couldn't keep my legs bent any more, they were trembling. The doctor could feel my shaking.

"It's okay, it's okay," he groaned, thumping karate chops on the backs of my thighs and forcing my knees to remain bent.

"I'm going to...I have to cross my legs or I'm going to..." I could barely speak.

"Nothing is going to happen!" the doctor snapped. "Just stand still till I've finished."

My breathing was out of control. I couldn't understand whether I should inhale or exhale. I was going to wet his hand any second if he wouldn't let me go to the toilet.

Then I coughed and choked and my thighs shut tightly around Dr. Doctor's fingers. He screamed. I screamed.

"Let go of my hand!" he shouted in panic. He beat on the back of my thighs to get me to open up my legs. I lost my balance and fell on top of him. The chair crashed to the ground. I hit the funny bone in my elbow and screamed again, shaking with laughter. My thighs released their precious cargo. The doctor pushed my body away, straightened his suit, and jammed my legs open with his knees. The sensations in my funny bone and the tingling between my legs felt like one and the same. I couldn't stop laughing.

"Crazy female!" the doctor panted, reaching up to grab one of the glass slides. He pushed my thighs further apart, almost tearing the muscle, then dug his finger again and again into my pouch of flesh and wiped his finger on the slide each time. Finally the doctor let go of my legs and I rolled over onto my side.

"Look!" commanded the doctor, pushing the slide under my nose. "I have captured your essence. Now we will get to the bottom of your too-tall self. They don't call me Dr. Doctor for nothing!"

He placed the second slide carefully over the first, sealing the secret of my too-tall body under the clear glass. He gulped down the coconut water, popped another sweet into his mouth and straightened his tie.

"Next week," he admonished, "you must do better. You must practice, practice, *practice*, until you learn to relax." Dr. Doctor slapped his palms together in prayer. "These are the fingers of a skilled surgeon," he hissed. "I cannot have you breaking them!"

I sat up slowly and looked around for my panties. They were under the desk. I grabbed them and slid them on. Dr. Doctor watched me while he popped another sweet into his mouth. His oily hair was plastered onto his forehead and his ears were bright red.

"What about my pouch of skin..."

"What's that?" snapped the doctor in irritation. "What did you say?"

"Inside. First it tickled, now it burns."

"Hmmm...," said the doctor, munching on more sweets. The box was now empty. He mashed the crumbs of sweets onto the end of one finger and licked it clean.

"Let it burn. No harm in it. You're a big girl now. You must learn to bear your pain."

Dr. Doctor brushed off his suit one last time, picked up his bag and walked out of the house.

I wondered whether I should tell my mother about this first session of treatment. At least now I knew what a *sexologist* did; I was certain that my mother did too. She must have known what female waters are, and how they affect a girl's height. She must also have known about the pouch of skin from where the female fluid flows. I resolved to tell her everything if she asked me, but the questions never came.

Perhaps she would get some hint of what was going on by spying on me through the door. The doctor had said to practice relaxing. I stood with my legs bent at the knees and tried to do what the doctor did. I tired quickly and achieved nothing. If my mother saw any of this through the keyhole, she made no mention of it.

A few days later, the doctor sent my mother his *diagnostic notes*, written out in beautiful handwriting:

INDICATIONS:
> *The patient has a tendency to immodesty and nakedness.*
> *The patient displays no resistance to contact with her female chamber.*
> *The patient produces fluid in overabundance, a condition normally seen only in Red-Light Women.*

DIAGNOSIS:
> *Coitus or other sexual stimulation will be deleterious to the patient's health.*

URGENT RECOMMENDATIONS:
> *Lifelong celibacy, supplemented by dedication to social causes.*
> *Early sterilization in case of accidental penetration.*
> *Further fluid samples from the patient for an ongoing, comprehensive evaluation.*

My mother stirred from her stupor. The tranquilizers kept her drowsy but her unhappiness penetrated the fog. Dr. Doctor's diagnostic notes mentioned nothing about a cure. My mother wanted results. She showed the doctor's letter to her friends. They were mildly disturbed at the extent of my problem, but were absolutely appalled at the recommendation that I remain unmarried and forcefully infertile. The sin to any woman of having an unmarried daughter in the house was just too much to bear.

Push for *results*, they told my mother. Don't get bullied into accepting his way of thinking. After all, he is a man, and cannot know what pain we go through. My mother decided that the doctor could test me three more times, and no more. Then she would take a look at his findings and send him on his way.

On the second visit, Dr. Doctor wore only an old short-sleeved shirt and floppy pants. Without his three-piece suit, he looked unimaginably thin. He rolled up his sleeves and smoothed back his hair, then looked around.

"Ah...no sweets for the doctor today?" he sighed wistfully.

"Water, if you like," I offered. The doctor was uninterested.

"How do you expect me to drink anything when I have to wrestle with you?" he retorted. "Have you been practicing how to relax?"

"I can lie down on the bed," I suggested. "That way we won't fall down."

"Hmph!" said Dr. Doctor. I removed my panties and lay back on the bed.

The doctor bent my legs at the knees, then pushed my thighs wide apart. I watched him pulling and pushing my body.

"Don't look at me!" he warned. He pulled a doctor's mask out of his pocket and slipped it onto his face, covering his nose and mouth.

"Have to be careful in unhealthy environments," he muttered, then bent down.

The doctor hunched down between my legs, digging in so hard that my belly danced in and out.

"I want to do it myself," I whispered, tracing his tense fingers with my own.

"Hmph!" he snorted and pushed my hand away. He resumed tickling me. I tried to bring my legs together, but he jammed his shoulder against one leg and stuck his elbow into the other.

"Relax!" he commanded. "I must do my job."

I could feel his fingers all the way to the knuckles, burrowing in me like worms. They were inside the pouch of skin, which was buried inside the mound of my belly, which was sunken inside the bag of my hips, which was buried inside the arms of the doctor. He was almost sitting on top of me.

The pouch of skin was like a fizzy Coke bottle. When he shook it, the fizz shot up and bubbled and spat and came sliding down into the bed and stained the sheets and wet the doctor's fingers. I could see the trail on the glass slide as he coated it with skin bottle fizz over and over again. As soon as he had finished, Dr. Doctor pulled off his mask, dropped the slides into his bag and snatched his payment off the cork board. He paused at the door.

"*I* am a licensed doctor, not you. God has given *me* these hands as tools, not you. It is my *duty* to stimulate your fluids! Disregard any inclinations towards contradicting that."

Ramdass found out from Lakshman that my mother had left me alone in the house with a stranger. Ramdass was anxious at the news and pressed me for details. Who was the man? Where did he come from? What did he do?

I chided Ramdass for being so stupid. I told him it was our *friend*, the one we saw every day when we went for the drive. Ramdass didn't know who I was referring to. He didn't remember ever seeing any man at Worli Sea Face. He blamed himself for buying the sweets without checking whom they were for.

"I thought Baby had invited another *baby* friend!"

I pointed out to Ramdass that he was my friend and *he* certainly wasn't a baby. Ramdass cried out in alarm at my words. He assured me that he was only the company driver, and if I went around calling him my friend, he would surely get into trouble.

When I got out of the car at the end of the day, Ramdass requested me to give him this Dr. Doctor's address. He said he would find out what kind of doctor-man he really was.

The doctor came for his third visit. By now he was dressed in tennis shorts and a t-shirt. His legs were like match sticks. He was as thin as a poor laborer.

I lay back on the bed and bent my knees. I opened them wide. Dr. Doctor nodded his approval.

"I've been thinking about our meeting," I volunteered, as he licked his fingers one by one and thrust them into me. I winced as I felt a jagged fingernail digging in at the opening.

"What's that?" he gasped, pressing his head between my legs. I could see only the back of his neck.

"I've known you for so long. Did you know that one day we would meet? Perhaps we were suddenly separated in a past life..."

My head swam as the doctor probed. I could feel the wetness through which his fingers slid like snakes. My knees folded in around the doctor's face and he jabbed me in the thigh.

"Pay attention!" he barked. "I don't have all day."

His fingers made me uncomfortable. His voice was too harsh. He was breaking the spell of our intimacy. I sat up suddenly, and his fingers slid right out. He looked at me in astonishment.

"*I'll* get the sample for you," I announced bravely.

"You are a *guest* in this house. This is too much work for you."

The doctor opened his mouth to contradict me, so I repeated, "You are a guest in this house. You must rest."

The doctor looked at me nervously. He wiped the sweat off his brow and stood up. I licked my finger and touched the opening of my pouch of skin. How unusual and soft it felt. I slid the tip of the finger through the sticky fluid spread all over between my legs. Everywhere I touched, my mouth let out a soft cry, like the meow of a cat. I was suddenly confused to be doing the doctor's job. I closed my eyes so I wouldn't see him frowning at me.

Soon my legs were trembling and shaking and the skin of my finger felt numb and puckered as though it had fallen asleep in a swimming pool. All in a rush, the mountain of skin rose up through me and pushed me down into the mattress. I could not move; the force of the moment sucked every ounce of strength out of me.

The doctor pushed away my useless hand and dug out the fluid. My skin burned where he touched me and my arms and legs jerked like puppets. His touch was too hard. I couldn't bear the pressure. I rolled over and shut my legs tightly. The feeling was very different now that *I* had done it. The doctor packed up his slides and left without a word.

I wondered whether I should tell my mother that I could now do to myself what the doctor was supposed to. She probably wouldn't care. She was busy looking for alternate solutions.

Ramdass quickly closed the car door for me, then slid into his seat. He pulled out onto the road with great speed. He spoke rapidly.

"This doctor of yours, he lives all alone at Worli Sea Face. No one visits him there. He sees all his patients in their homes. All of them are memsahibs and girls of good family like you. Many of them have remained his patients for ten, fifteen, twenty years."

I remained silent, so Ramdass turned to me in alarm.

"Don't you see, Baby?" he pleaded. "This man is good-for-nothing. What kind of doctor keeps his patients sick forever?"

"Tell my mother," I replied casually.

Ramdass stepped hard on the brakes and I fell forward against the seat. He pulled over to the side of the road and turned to me.

"Please, Baby, I am a good man. I come and go quietly every day. I do my job properly and I respect your father and mother. Please don't get me into any trouble. I cannot speak directly to your mother or anyone else in your family. All blame will fall on my head. I am a man and I know how men are. I am simply telling you what I have found out."

I imagined Ramdass as a detective, sneaking around the doctor's office with his peaked driver's cap pulled low over his eyes, looking furtively through the files, coaxing information out of the building lift man, bribing the doctor's peon to spill his secrets. I smiled with satisfaction. Ramdass was a true friend.

"Very good, Ramdass," I said in my stiffest memsahib tone. "You are a good worker and I will recommend you for a raise."

Ramdass shook his head sadly and put the car into gear.

"How will you understand, Baby. I don't care about the money. You are still young. I have done what I can. Now I leave it to god."

I listened to the concern in Ramdass's voice. He was such a loyal companion.

"The doctor knows something about me that you don't," I confessed to Ramdass. "You didn't find out anything about that, did you?"

Ramdass frowned into the rearview mirror.

"No," he finally admitted. "I didn't."

"Did you enjoy being a detective?" I asked.

Ramdass's sad face suddenly twitched and then he burst out laughing.

"Yes, Baby, I really did enjoy myself!" Ramdass paused, suddenly thoughtful. "I looked everywhere in his house, but only one thing I didn't find was his doctor's bag. That man must keep evil things in his bag, I just know it."

I thought of the slides sitting wrapped in the doctor's bag. What would Ramdass make of them? He would look at them over and over, puzzling over them, turning them this way and that. Would he finally lift off the top slide and smell the liquid? Would he finally realize what it was and cry out, *Baby?*

The thought of it made me smile.

My mother waited out the doctor's third visit, then on a school morning she called up and informed the principal's office that I would be absent from lessons that day. She took her time dressing me up in one of her silk saris, tied my hair back in a bun, applied some lipstick to my face and splashed me with perfume.

I inspected myself in the mirror. I had been transformed! I looked like a grown woman. How did I get this way? My mother solemnly fixed her hair and straightened her sari, and we left the house.

Ramdass paled as he saw me walk toward the car. He looked nervously from me to my mother but said nothing. He got into the car and started the engine. When he looked back at me through the rearview mirror, I could tell he was frightened. I shrugged as if to ask him *What?* and he looked even more unhappy.

We drove to the Taj Mahal Hotel. Ramdass let us off in front and we walked up the steps into the dazzling lobby. The chandeliers glinted and sparkled in the midday sun. The hushed tones of foreigners filled the large carpeted space. There were Arab men in long white robes, blond giants in jeans and t-shirts, chic Indian women in heavily embroidered silk suits. Different perfumes mingled in the cool air. My mother had me sit in the first empty seat, so that my height wouldn't cause too many heads to turn. She left me there as she went to find the person we had come to meet.

Two European men watched my mother cross to the front desk, then turned to face me. They looked at me and smiled. Immediately I lowered my eyes, but then I wondered why.

Why couldn't I look at a tall blond man? I had stared into the doctor's eyes for years. I had looked at Ramdass all my life. These men were no different. Green eyes instead of brown, that's all. Why should anyone stop me?

I looked up in triumph and the two foreigners immediately stood up and came over. My mother came racing back across the lobby.

"Watch out!" she shouted in warning.

The two men stepped back as my mother came to a stop by my chair. They scowled in defeat and walked away.

"You see," my mother breathed conspiratorially. "Everyone thinks you're a grown woman. That's why I've brought you here. This Engineer will fix up something for you."

My mother couldn't find an empty seat near me, so she sat on a sofa across from me, glaring at all the men who sauntered past my chair.

We sat in the lobby and waited for Mrs. Engineer to come down from her room. She was getting her massage. She came to Bombay twice a year, by appointment only. She always stayed at the Taj. She traveled to all the big cities in India, and also to London, New York and Toronto.

A large woman wearing a shimmering sari of white and gold silk waddled out of the lift. She had short curled hair and beamed from ear to ear. My mother jumped up and waved at her. Mrs. Engineer nodded and came bouncing towards us. My mother stood by my side and clasped my shoulder tightly.

"Aha!" Mrs. Engineer beamed by way of greeting. "What have we here!" She tugged on my hand to get me to stand up, but my mother pressed down firmly on my shoulder.

"Later," my mother whispered nervously. "You can see her deformity when we leave."

Mrs. Engineer took my mother's hand and chided her gently.

"Do not use that word, madam. Each of us is one of god's children. I give you my oath that we will find a suitable match for her. Our service has been very successful, as you know. How else could I afford to stay in this hotel?" Mrs. Engineer swept her arm across the majestic lobby. My mother nodded glumly.

"In India, no one needs to be left out of matrimony. We guarantee a match. Now I will tell you all the groups we work with day in and day out." Mrs. Engineer took a deep breath.

"We have married," she sang at the top of her voice, "the blind...the deaf...the frigid...diabetics...amputees...midgets... mental patients...black-skinned girls...alcoholics...women of the night...and also giants, like your daughter." Mrs. Engineer had a twinkle in her eye.

"All this, of course, as long as you are willing to pay."

Mrs. Engineer burped contentedly and looked from my mother to me.

"For an extra fee, very small really, we can teach your daughter how to cook, clean, sew, give her husband massage and other womanly things. We guarantee marriage for your child, but cannot promise a servant in the house to do the work for her!"

My mother blanched and gripped the chair.

"You mean...my darling..."

"I assure you, madam, we will arrange for your daughter to marry as far from Bombay as possible, and you need never see the man or the conditions in which he lives. Soon your daughter will adjust because, after all, she will be a respectable married woman and have children and a husband to take care of. Our service has a ninety percent success rate, especially when you send some extra money each month to guarantee that the husband treats the girl well."

"But...but...but..." My mother was agitated by the thought of me down on my knees, scrubbing the floor, bending over the well, drawing up buckets of water, blowing on the coals between gusts of smoke, coughing over a cooking fire.

Mrs. Engineer clapped her hands to silence the whimpering.

"Mrs. Mehta!" she barked. "Let us not mince words. Your daughter has a visible *deformity*. The whole world can see it. Nothing you can do will change her problem. I am very disappointed by your attitude. As her mother, it is *your duty* to get her married. I leave Bombay at the end of the week. I expect to see sufficient down payment delivered to my room before then. Now goodbye!"

Mrs. Engineer stood where she was, glaring at us. My mother hoped she would walk away, but the matchmaker wanted a glimpse of my height. My mother took her hand off my shoulder and walked quickly out of the lobby. I stood up and straightened my sari. The hem fell short, brushing at my ankles when it had stretched down to my toes on arrival. My body had increased in length yet again. Mrs. Engineer watched me wiggle my body as I slid the sari lower down around my hips. She clapped her hands together in glee and chuckled.

"Take good care of yourself," Mrs. Engineer warbled. "You are worth your *height* in gold to me."

The next morning Ramdass drove me to school. I started crying in the back seat and Ramdass immediately pulled over to the side of the road. He bit his lips, scratched his head and wrung his hands.

"Baby," he said softly, "very sorry, Baby. You are in pain? You want to go home?"

I shook my head. Ramdass sat in silence, watching me stretched out on the back seat with my face in my hands.

"No. Don't do anything. Don't go anywhere. You're my only friend. Just stay with me."

Ramdass smiled nervously and shook his head.

"What kind of friend can I be? I am stupid, only a driver. Who is friends with a fool like me?"

Ramdass turned off the engine and we sat in silence, listening to the cars rushing by. I looked at Ramdass as he stared out of the window. He had the kindest face I had ever seen.

"Where are you from?" I asked him.

"Very far away, Baby, my village is on the other side of India."

"Where is your wife?"

"She has gone to heaven, poor woman, so many years ago. I left my children with my mother and came to this city to find work."

"You have a house in the village?"

"It is only a hut. We are simple village people."

Ramdass turned to face me, uncertain about my inquiries. In all the years he had worked for us, I had never asked him any personal questions. He let his hand hang over the back of his seat.

I took his hand in mine. He gasped and tried to pull away but I clasped his hand hard. His skin was smooth with calluses.

"I am going to marry you, Ramdass. You don't have to treat me in any special way and we don't have to have children. You don't even have to make a woman of me: I know how to take care of all of that. We will go back to your village and live with your family. My parents will send lots of money which will take care of all of us."

Ramdass cried out as though I had struck him and jerked his hand away. He shrank back against the steering wheel, then jumped backwards out of the car as though his seat were on fire. He put his arms around his body and shivered miserably. He squatted on the ground and clasped his head between his hands. He was very afraid.

I hadn't stopped to think that Ramdass might not want me. He *had* to save me! Didn't he care for me? He had known me since I was a child, and must have always loved me. Now he simply had to learn to love me as a *wife*.

It struck me that I might yet get Ramdass under my spell. I reached forward and honked the horn. Ramdass stood up slowly and brushed off his uniform. He got into the car and sat slumped over the wheel. I tapped him gently on the shoulder.

"If you won't marry me," I whispered, "at least stop the doctor from stealing my essence. You don't want him to keep me sick forever."

Ramdass stiffened and lifted his head.

"Why do you let him into the house? Call the police! They will arrest him."

"Ramdass, you know that no one listens to a young girl. If you do it my way, we won't get into any trouble. This evening after the doctor leaves our house, follow him. As soon as you can, open his bag and take everything out carefully. There you will find what he steals from me. He seals it between two pieces of glass. You will recognize what it is. Bring it back to me."

Ramdass breathed deeply and his shoulders relaxed. He started the car engine and nodded thoughtfully. He was back to being his old self.

"That bad man has stolen something of yours. Ramdass, company driver, will bring it back!"

Twenty minutes before the doctor's fourth visit, I pulled off my panties and lay down on the bed. I could feel that my female fluid was already leaking out. I slowly massaged the loose skin all around my pouch of skin. By now I knew that what I felt down there was not ordinary, even though this was simply my body touching my own body.

When the doctor walked in, the skin fizz was already spread out and cooling between my legs. He saw from my face that I had finished his job. I stretched my glistening fingers toward him. Without a word he gave me the glass slide.

Is this what kept his other patients sick for ten or twenty years? Letting him take their fluids week after week, touching them where no one else ever did. I turned away from him and reached in to wipe up the fluid with my fingers. I could feel his eyes burning into my side. I could no longer look into the doctor's eyes with the old thrill of anticipation. I could no longer match him stare for stare. I suddenly realized that it didn't matter if I never saw him again.

I loaded up the slide with the familiar sticky liquid, but then saw with surprise that there was a curly hair mixed in. I felt around with my fingers and realized that I hadn't even noticed that there was hair growing between my legs. Where had it come from!

I put the wet slide on Dr. Doctor's palm. He placed the second slide on top of the first, wrapped the two in tissue paper, tossed the bundle into his bag and snapped it shut. The envelope with his payment remained pinned to the cork board.

"You don't have to come back here anymore," I murmured.

The doctor turned sharply at my words. His eyes were wide with anger.

"What exactly do you mean? Does your mother know what you've decided?"

"It's my mother who doesn't want you here." I shrugged. "She has another plan for me."

The doctor smoothed his hair back and snarled. He pulled his payment off the cork board and tore the envelope in half.

"Ungrateful ignorant women," he muttered hatefully. "You won't get rid of me so easily." Dr. Doctor marched out of the house.

I ran to the window that overlooked the spot where Ramdass was parked. The doctor hailed a taxi on the street, and Ramdass slowly pulled out behind him. The chase was on! I crossed my fingers tightly and wished the driver best of luck.

All that evening I thought about Ramdass. We would get married, but he would surely want me to complete my schooling. Perhaps he could continue as a driver for a few more years, or perhaps there was a good school in the village where he lived.

If Ramdass's house was small, then he would have little furniture. Ramdass, his mother, his children and I would all sit cross-legged on the ground and eat out of metal plates. What kind of food did he like? He probably loved chilies, and I would have to learn to like them as well.

Would his mother choose to change my name, giving me a new identity as the lucky young bride? Would she lock our bedroom door from the outside for our first night as was common with a newly married couple?

I saw myself lying on the bed next to Ramdass, both of us buried under mounds of nuptial flowers. From the corner of my eye I saw that Ramdass was afraid. I heard him excusing himself for not touching me. After his wife's death he had made a vow before god that he would never touch another woman again. I heard myself telling Ramdass not to worry, I already knew how to touch myself and didn't need him for any of that. I saw Ramdass relax at those words and put his palms together in gratitude. I teased him that he could watch me if he wanted, and he laughed with delight. I heard him say that he always knew that Baby was a clever girl.

It was close to dinnertime. Perhaps the doctor was out for a stroll or visiting friends for a meal. Ramdass would make his move, enter the doctor's house and search out the medical bag. He would carefully pull out the contents one by one, puzzling over each one of them as he had no familiarity with a doctor's tools. Out would come the stethoscope, prescription pad, cotton wool, syringes, face masks, gloves. Stuffed in the middle would be empty sweet wrappers, calling cards, pens, pencils, notebooks. And there to one side would be the slim package of glass slides wrapped in tissues.

Ramdass would think about this. The other items in the bag were solid, functional. This item was wrapped. It was different. He would unroll the tissue and pull out the slides. He would see the smear of liquid, but not feel any wetness on the top or bottom. Turning the slides on their side would reveal that there were two joined together. Ramdass would carefully slide a nail between the slides and pry them apart. There would be a soft sucking noise as the slides came clear of each other.

Ramdass would stare at the bottom slide cautiously, then bring it to his nose. He would smell my fluid and gasp. He would recognize the smell as belonging to me. It would take a while for him to understand that he was now under my spell. But then he would draw in my aroma once again and declare his love for me. There was a sudden banging on my bedroom door. "Get up, come out, the doctor is here!" shouted my mother. I jumped off my bed and unlocked the room door with shaking hands. I pulled the door open. Ramdass stood sobbing in front of me, utterly defeated. I screamed and withdrew into my room. Dr. Doctor gave a grim smile and stepped in after me. My mother followed him in, her eyes flashing with rage.

Dr. Doctor walked up and down the room, lost in thought. "Sit, sit," he told my mother and me. We sat on the bed. Dr. Doctor pulled Ramdass into the room and pressed him down to the floor until he collapsed cross-legged. Dr. Doctor wiped his hands on his jacket and cleared his throat.

"I encountered this man in my house. I asked him who he was and what he wanted. I shouted at him to get out, but he gave no response. He had spread all the contents of my medical bag onto a table and was standing over the mess crying wretchedly. In his hand was the fluid sample I had collected in this very house a few hours earlier."

Dr. Doctor paused, and looked at me. I looked back at him, trying to ascertain how much he really knew. My mother couldn't believe what she was hearing.

"Ramdass broke into your house? But he would never do such a thing. He doesn't even know where you live!" The doctor ignored her interruption.

"I took this wretch aside and I asked him what the devil he thought he was doing. He started babbling about someone named Baby. He said he had to find her a good husband, that he couldn't marry her, he just couldn't do it, he kept babbling about not doing it."

Ramdass had given me away!

My face burned with horror. I looked at the driver, willing him to lift his head and deny everything, but of course Ramdass didn't understand any English.

"When I asked him why the devil he was in tears, he pointed to the specimen slide, which has, of all things, a pubic hair on it. He said that he couldn't live with himself now that he had seen Baby's nakedness. Imagine, a grown man crying over a pubic hair!"

My mother stood up unsteadily and tried to form some words but her mouth wouldn't obey. She walked to the window and leaned her ashen face on the glass. The doctor looked at her witheringly and continued.

"I figured out that this chap was your driver, and that Baby is none other than your specimen daughter. I realized that some plan involving marriage is obviously afoot, against my better recommendations. I can see however that you don't have any great ambitions if you're going to marry her off to this...this *driver!*"

At the word "driver," Ramdass looked up. He looked directly at me with his kind eyes and spoke sadly.

"Baby, I cannot make you happy in this world. I am a poor man who knows nothing. But this Doctor sahib, he is a good man who can treat you with honor. Why not let *him* take care of you? He has a big house, a good job and no wife. How could I ever compare with him. I am a man and I know how men are; he will make a better husband for you."

"Ramdass!" my mother screamed out his name and looked at him in amazement. I covered my ears, anticipating a torrent of rage directed at the driver. But my mother was speechless with a different emotion: gratitude. Her lips quivered hopefully and her eyes brimmed with joy. She turned to Dr. Doctor.

"Doctor...," she groaned, her hands forming question marks in the air. "Could it be true?"

My mother bit her tongue as soon as the words came out, but she willed herself to continue.

"Would you really marry my daughter? Can god in heaven be so kind?"

Dr. Doctor looked at me triumphantly from the corner of his eye. He opened his arms expansively and then joined his hands in humble prayer.

"I took an oath as a physician. It is my duty to heal. Where I cannot change the ways of nature in mending your daughter's body, at least I can offer my humble self as husband and protector of her womanhood."

I could not believe what was being said in front of me. My mind was playing tricks on me.

The driver spoke with my mother's voice.

"Oh doctor," he gushed, "god will bless you for accepting this deformed girl as your wife."

The doctor spoke with my mother's voice.

"She should consider herself lucky. She may be too tall, but after all she isn't a *blackie*."

My mother spoke with the driver's voice.

"A husband for Baby! It is very good. We must buy sweets to welcome him into our home."

My head rang like a vibrating metal gong. My skin crawled as though covered with ants. My face burned as though too close to a fire.

My mother swayed back and forth while crying with relief, squeezing the doctor's palm with one hand and brushing off the driver's uniform with the other. She told Ramdass how time after time she had defended him to her husband, insisting that the driver be maintained in their employ as he was such a trustworthy fellow. She told Dr. Doctor how she had sensed right from the beginning when given his name that he was the man for her daughter.

My limbs suddenly itched. My skin felt like it was stretching. My body was going to reach farther away from the people of the world and grow taller right there and then, even though I was already bigger than everyone I knew. They called me *jumbo* and *demon, giant* and *mutant*. I was not one of them! I was not one of them and I never *had* to be.

"Stop!" I screamed at my limbs and at my mother.

"Stop it now!" I cried to my bones and to the driver.

"Don't you dare do it," I spat vehemently at my body and at the doctor.

I felt the pressure ease in my joints and a relaxing of my skin.

"None of you can decide for me. None of you. I know what I am. Not you."

I felt the tautness release in my bones and a slackening in my flesh.

"I am not an animal. I do not belong to you. I am not a slave. I am not scared of you."

I felt a warm glow light up my body and a cool breeze fan my brain.

"Don't you understand that I'm bigger than all of you? Get out of here. Get out at once. Get out!"

I knew right then without a doubt that my body would no longer grow.

Tears of Kamala

Kamala cries a hundred tears every day. Her tears mark the length of the day, from sunrise to sunset.

"It's good to cry," her mother would say when Kamala came running with a bleeding cut. Kamala would look at her mother wide-eyed, then squeeze her face tight into a scowl and grunt a few times. In this way she would be done with expressing her pain before her mother had even swabbed the wound.

Immediately her mother would slap her across the face.

"If it doesn't hurt, you don't have to cry. But don't show disrespect. All other children cry when they hurt themselves."

"But the tears burn, amma. They don't want to come."

"So what if they burn? Doesn't vomit burn? When your stomach is sick and wants to throw the food out, you don't keep it in just because it burns."

Kamala is standing on the bus as she does every day, holding onto the warm moist straps that hang from the roof of the roaring single-decker. A voice is shouting at her, but Kamala doesn't see where it is coming from. She glances at the passengers, who are all beseeching her silently. Every woman looks at Kamala with fearful eyes. The shouting voice is insistent.

"Madam, please do not humiliate me in front of the whole world. Take the seat, I beg of you!"

An anguished man tugs on Kamala's arm and points at the empty seat directly in front of her. He looks as though he will sob at any moment. Kamala shakes her head and puts her finger to her lips.

"Ssshh!" says Kamala. She counts the number to herself.

51

The tear is heavy and hot, like a small burning coal. Kamala closes her eyes. The drop slides down excruciatingly slowly, lingering as though wanting to drag her skin along with it. It stops for a moment as though refusing to move further, gathers in its trailing moisture, then drops with an almost audible hiss onto the over-heated floor of the bus. Kamala steps back to take a look. There it is! The opaque drop glistens on the studded metal floor, then races under the nearest seat as the bus swings around a corner.

The man implores Kamala with his eyes. The other passengers bend forward with radiant curiosity. There is one empty seat on the bus, and the man wants Kamala to take it. Kamala turns to him, wide-eyed.

"Sir, you are obviously new on this bus and ignorant of my

ways. I stand at work, I stand at home, I stand on the bus. I don't sit. You are wasting your time."

Kamala turns away from the man and walks to the very front of the bus, pulling herself forward on the hanging straps. Hers is the next stop.

52

This time Kamala feels the burning trail of the tear begin deep inside her, in a place she never feels at other times. It is surprising to her that the inside of her body does, after all, register strong feeling. The tear is like a drop of acid or a pebble of dry ice.

The bus jerks and swerves as the driver weaves around pedestrians crossing through the moving traffic. The driver presses on the horn as a stout mother in a stiff sari casually pulls her young sons behind her. The matron brazenly holds up her hand, signaling the bus driver to stop. He continues hurtling towards her. At the last minute he changes lanes and pulls in to the curb. The bus screeches to a halt and Kamala walks down the steps.

53

She quickly looks behind her and sees that the tear has fallen on the bottom step. An elderly gentleman in a suit and spotless shoes steps down right behind Kamala and slips on the drop. He howls in alarm and is propelled forward onto Kamala. Kamala turns to him with her finger on her lips.

"Ssshh!" she cautions him.

54

This tear speeds down. The old man takes his time disengaging himself from contact with Kamala's person. The man smirks at having unexpectedly achieved full bodily contact with a woman. He brushes off his sleeves and straightens his tie as a dozen more passengers quickly alight from the bus. The man turns to Kamala.

"Very sorry, madam," he snickers, looking her up and down.

"Hooligans spit anywhere nowadays, even on the steps of a B.E.S.T. bus! This city has gone to the dogs."

Kamala straightens the shoulder of her sari, smiles briefly at the old man, then walks towards the street crossing. The man follows her with greedy eyes. As soon as she is out of earshot, he blows her a long squealing kiss wet with saliva.

Kamala works as a cashier in a bank at Nariman Point, one of the busiest areas of Bombay. Thousands of clerks, secretaries and other office staff walk rapidly down the streets towards their workplaces. Kamala is carried along in the crowd as she crosses the street, propelled along as though bodily linked with the forms of the sweating, grunting, perfumed women on either side of her.

55

At these moments there is a lot of contact against Kamala's skin—arms pressing against arms, elbows jabbing at her stomach, footwear striking at her heels. Kamala prefers to focus only on the next tear pouring thickly out of her. In order to do so she has already shut her skin off from the outside world. It is very easy for her to do this. She inhales deeply, then tenses all the muscles of her body with one powerful squeeze that whips through her body like the cosmically uncoiled snake. Such force would normally knock a body to the ground, but in the rushing crowds that stream past her apartment building every morning, Kamala wedges herself in tightly and shocks her body into submission. As she moves with the thousands to catch her bus, she transforms into a safely cushioned sleepwalker, her skin miraculously free of all impression.

"It's good to cry," her mother-in-law had said to Kamala after her first month of marriage. Kamala had gone sleepless for thirty nights. Her wide eyes were sunken into her face, hardened inside circles of skin as dark as the shells of coconuts.

"Women's tears are the spring of life. Where they fall, there the parched earth sends up shoots. It is no different for your parched body. Cry now and water yourself, or you will dry up too soon."

But Kamala was already shedding tears, though her mother-in-law didn't know. What Kamala coveted was the sleep of the dead that freed her from the persistence of memory and allowed her to start afresh each day.

Lying at night on the thin mattress that separated her from the floor, she tensed all her muscles with one immense contraction that convulsed her body as though tossed up by an electrical storm. In this way Kamala mastered the process of shutting off her skin, and immediately she was able to recover her sleep.

56

The tear falls on the smooth walkway leading to the bank. The surface is polished and slick. Kamala quickly smears the tear on the sole of her sandal, lest another man slip on it. She arrives at the door of the bank and glances at the sentry standing menacingly in front of it.

57

The man is a guard! He does not move. Kamala panics. Who is this man? Where has he come from?

A moment later he nods in greeting and steps to one side of the glass door trimmed with gold. Kamala realizes he is the same guard who stands there every morning. The last tear happened to fall right at the moment when her eyes met his, and the burning liquid temporarily played havoc with her mind.

Kamala enters the building and immediately the outside world is shut out. The bank is air-conditioned and has a gleaming marble floor. The ceiling is very high, and the distant sounds of footsteps, typewriters and shuffled papers bounce back and forth across the room. It is like being underwater. Kamala shuffles her feet on the doormat, wiping the soles of her sandals clean.

58

The tear falls on the thick hairs of the coir mat, and is immediately absorbed into the dry fiber. So many tears! Every day of her married life. They are impossible to ignore, so Kamala acknowledges and harvests them, counting them out until the last tear has descended. Finally Kamala can release her skin back to sensation, and for a few precious hours her body revels again in the endlessly shifting waves of physical feeling.

59

Kamala could stand on the coir mat all day watching her tears being absorbed, but the bank is about to open and Kamala has to set up her window. She quickly crosses over to the line of cashiers' cubicles and pulls open the iron gate that separates the employees from the customers. She walks rapidly behind the screen of glass panes alternating with barred grilles until she arrives at her own window which is seventh in the row of eight. She slips the key into her cashier's drawer.

60

At her cash counter, Kamala feels relaxed because here she can stand in dignity and let the tears gather around. Kamala's counter space has no chair or stool as she prefers to stand.

When she first joined the bank, Kamala was too timid to request that her chair be removed, so she squeezed herself in between the chair and the counter and stood in that cramped space all day. It was only several months after Kamala had been with the bank that the manager noticed how Kamala never used her chair. The manager was exasperated.

"Sit, sit, or you will become a bad worker, tired all the time. Unnecessarily you'll get varicose veins. What do you expect us to do with this chair? Send it to the Queen of England?"

Kamala suggested that the bank customers might like a chair

to sit on while awaiting their turn. The manager grumbled about her ingratitude and threatened to have her disciplined. The following day, however, the chair was gone.

61

The tear springs out while Kamala is counting out her cash drawer and she is distracted. She giggles at the image of 61 branded into her mind, then quickly recounts the money and signs her name in the cash ledger.

She taps the metal bell on the counter and immediately the sound rings and echoes through the high-ceilinged bank. A tea-boy is already making his way to her cubicle with a glass of steaming chai in his hand. He bangs the glass down on the counter and the hot liquid swirls alarmingly towards the rim with the force of one of her tears, but then subsides without overflowing. Kamala wonders what would happen if she could force her tears to remain contained within her like the tea within the glass.

62

Only thirty-eight tears left. Kamala anticipates the joy of counting out the last one when the agitating receptors of her skin will suddenly spring to life from their twice-daily dormancy.

The cashiers' cubicles fill up one by one. On Kamala's left at the last window in the row stands Ramanathan. He is a recent B. Comm. graduate who is painfully thin but nonetheless wears extra-tight drainpipe trousers. His tiny bird-like face is overwhelmed by a bushy mustache composed of twisting upright hairs that often tickle Ramanathan in the nose and make his face twitch like a mouse. No matter how vigorously he smoothes them down, the hairs of his mustache stick out like hastily snipped wires. The female cashiers laugh at him behind his back, calling him names like *Pipe Cleaner*, *Shoe Brush* and *Welcome Mat*. Ramanathan is the only male cashier at the bank.

63

Kamala can feel that this tear is particularly heavy and sad. The drop drags the old sorrow out of her. She yearns to feel lighter.

On Kamala's right sits Fiona, an Anglo-Indian who commutes from Bandra. Fiona speaks English like an elocution teacher, stretching and pouting her lips to enunciate every syllable. She files her nails while customers fill out the numerous slips and forms so essential to bank work.

Fiona does not speak to Kamala unless she has to and Ramanathan is too shy to say a word, so on most days Kamala engages only in brief conversations with customers which leaves her relatively free to concentrate on counting tears.

64

Each tear that falls rings a register in her head, big white numbers just like on the old-fashioned tills where the thick digits roll into place when the number keys are banged and thumped.

65

Each tear drips away the hours between sunrise and sunset. Kamala's body is like a diurnal faucet: open and leaking during the day; closed and contained at night.

The bank is now open. The guard steps away from the entrance and the crowd of anxious customers rush in. They dart from cashier to cashier as though playing musical chairs, hoping to be the first or second in line. Already they are jumping up to catch the eye of the cashiers, tapping impatiently on their watch faces, pushing and puffing in exasperation.

66

Sometimes when the numbers ring in her mind's eye, Kamala is staring at the face of a customer. The number is then imprinted on the customer's face. *You're 63! 79! 84!* she giggles to herself. Whenever these customers return to her window, their imprinted numbers spring up in Kamala's mind, and she can identify them as easily as if they were members of a beloved sports team.

67

Kamala plants herself in exactly the right position from which she can receive and dispense money and receipts at her window without actually shifting the trunk of her body. She sometimes feels the desire to see all her tears accumulate in a pile in one spot. In this way she can feel herself lightening with the physical evidence of tears gathering beneath her.

68

The tears are beginning to fall slower now. The customers rush in and out of the bank, forming a wave of constant motion like confetti dancing in the breeze. Only the tears retain their concrete solid forms.

69

The tears have slowed to a snail's pace. The tension of welcoming the next one into the air-conditioned air is almost too much to bear. Kamala thinks, it's a good thing that the tears don't *enter* me as slowly as they crawl out!

70

Kamala lifts the hem of her sari and peers cautiously down at the marble floor. Ah-ha! The tears have indeed gathered in one single pile like half-melted wax. They will remain wet as long as the next one falls right on top. If Kamala wishes, she can scrape the soft opaque mound onto a large leaf and hand it to the temple priests who present the offering of devotees to the gods. Once blessed, the offering transforms into prasad, sacred food. Kamala knows that she would be the only one possessing prasad of tears.

Ramanathan burps loudly several times in succession and Kamala is startled by the noise.

71

The tear zooms out of her. Kamala doesn't dare look to see if it has missed the mark. She glares at Ramanathan, but he is busy helping a customer. Ramanathan's burps indicate that all of his breakfast has been digested, right in time to free up his stomach for lunch.

72

Kamala feels a sudden anxiety in the pit of her stomach. She hates the lunch hour. She cannot eat or drink while the tears are flowing, cannot empty her bladder or her bowel. There is nothing for her to do during lunch, and no colleague or customer on whom to concentrate her energy. She can only count her tears.

73

The guard slams shut the door of the bank and locks it from the inside. The sudden noise surprises another tear out of Kamala, but after springing out so quickly, it sits on her skin. Reluctantly it blazes a downward trail. The sloth with which it travels is nerve-wracking.

The cashiers burst into sudden chatter, scraping back their stools and chairs, locking their cash drawers, closing their thick ledgers. Within seconds, everyone has disappeared into the lunch room, and the bank is gradually enveloped in a cloud of silence.

74

Kamala stands trembling at her counter. She can't control the shaking. She blinks her eyes open and shut with such force that her eyeballs hurt. She tries to bat away the sudden onslaught of images that have been tightly contained since the previous night.

Kamala claps one hand over her eyes and stuffs the end of her sari into her mouth. She chews on the cloth with great gulping mouthfuls of air, trying to stop the quivering in her belly.

75

This too will pass, Kamala knows. Only twenty-five more to go! She thumps her fist violently on the counter top, reciting to herself, Only twenty-five more! Only twenty-five more to one hundred when I am reborn again into my own body, without hidden chambers, without secret compartments, without an unfeeling outside that shelters the unbelieving inside. Only twenty-five more to go...

Every night, like a bird without wings that lies pinned to the earth, she waits for him. He comes late at night after dinner and liquor. He refuses to take food from her. He comes home to sleep, but in that house he can no longer sleep because she steals his sleep from him. The moment he enters the house, she shuts off her skin. The shock of the effort whips through her, uncoiling the snake at the base of her spine to stand guard against sensation. Her body floods with comforting numbness.

She must release her body or he will break her bones with his hatred. She must release her body or he will tear her skin off in handfuls. She must release her body or he will pulverize her into dust with the burden of his weight, grinding her down and down into the flattened cotton mattress that dips down into the sagging wooden floor.

She doesn't wear glass bangles because he would effortlessly crush the bits into her skin. She doesn't wear a necklace because he would willingly drive the stones into her skull. She won't wear her cotton sari because he tears it to shreds. She wears only the damp cotton towel that conceals her face under a curtain of dark moistness that keeps his breath from suffocating her, that keeps his eyes from devouring her.

Every night like a hunter lost in an unknown wood, the man stalks the wingless bird. He never tires of hurtling himself onto her and pinning her like a fearsome beast. He never tires of slamming his elbows deep into her armpits until he jars the bone. He never wearies of kicking her legs apart as though they are goal posts erected to concentrate his every attack.

Every night he invokes one greedy hand to undo his pants and the other to corral her neck.

*"Tonight, I **will** make you cry!"*

But the wingless bird is far inside the armor of her body where numbness shields her from the hunter's harm.

"Cry!" he screams at her every night. "Cry for me, woman, show me big juicy tears. I work hard to make you feel, I work hard to make you a woman. Cry for me like I cry for you from my big blind eye, these tears that go right up inside of you where they belong. My tears of manhood must nourish your parched belly that neither births nor bleeds. How many tears have I cried in you! How many oceans of tears have I wasted on you!"

By the time the wingless bird counts from one to ten, the hunter has fallen off her. She can almost count each of his man's tears racing like marbles to hide in the soft wide cushion of her womb.

The prey of the hunter faints into sleep. The tears work furiously in her all night, but to no avail. At sunrise, the first tear is ready to leave and brims impatiently at the mouth of her opening.

When the wingless bird awakes, she senses light in the room. Her body tingles with the sensations of morning. She savors the freedom to feel once again and removes the towel from her face. Her body is covered by a sheet. She does not remember the hunter lying next to her, spent. She does not recollect how quickly he pulls his own clothes on to hide his intense shame. She does not recall how fearfully he scrambles across the room looking for a sheet to cover her nakedness. Even as the sword of the hunt is kept in a sheath, so too the victim of the hunt is kept under a veil.

When both male and female are finally covered, his courage returns. "Die in your sleep," he curses her and leaves the house once again.

Afternoons in the bank pass slowly. Kamala's colleagues keep a curious eye on her and by the four o'clock tea break everyone notices that Kamala has turned very pale. They all speculate about her, wondering when she will finally stop acting strange.

Fiona reports that she has seen a few brown sugar addicts, and they behave just the way Kamala does. Energetic and capable while the brown sugar flows through their veins, they get sickly and withdrawn once the dose wears off.

"Pathetic addict," sniffs Fiona. "How dare she work in our bank."

"On the other hand," counters Monisha, the plump mother from Lamington Road, "perhaps Kamala is religious and keeps a fast during lunch as a prayer for her family."

"But we are *paying* her to eat lunch!" the manager exclaims with annoyance. "Let her keep a fast on holidays. This thankless female simply won't learn the value of money."

Reshma, the petite cashier from Byculla whispers that Kamala never has her monthly bleeding.

"My god!" shrieks Fiona. "Kamala must be a man dressed up as a woman!"

Ramanathan presses down on his mustache and contradicts Fiona with an ingratiating smile.

"I am knowing that Missus Kamala is a woman because," and there he stops to twirl his mustache triumphantly, "if you get close to her, you can *smell* that she is consummating with some gent *every day.* "

Ramanathan's indiscreet comment embarrasses the group into silence. They finish their tea marveling at the wonderful world they live in where even a strange creature like Kamala is rewarded with a virile husband who dutifully services his wife every day.

The last three drops fall between five and six o'clock. It is a time of unbearable tension for Kamala as she anticipates the arousal of her numbed sensations. The last drop often falls as she steps out of the bank. Suddenly her bladder and bowel exert such painful pressure that she turns around and walks back into the bank, holding up her pinkie to the alarmed sentry.

In the bathroom, the rush of relief almost causes her to pass out. Her heart flutters unsteadily as she draws on primordial survival strength to put herself back into motion and make it through the door of the bank.

As the door locks shut behind her, Kamala is ravaged by hunger and thirst. Just a few steps in front of her is the snack seller's stall where freshly fried foods are dished onto metal plates and handed out to the thronging customers. Kamala propels herself forward to the shaded booth and grabs a plate of samosas. She stuffs the fat triangular shapes into her mouth, savoring the warmth of the potato filling. She licks up the red chili sauce and grabs yet another plate of samosas which she washes down with spicy hot tea, followed by a tumblerful of ice water and then a sticky sweet ice cream. Slowly her body regains life.

At some point the stall owner cranes his neck through the crowd of customers and recognizes Kamala's glowing face. He has a round brown face and a perpetual smile. He greets her with a laugh and a shout, and Kamala acknowledges him with a vigorous nod. The snack seller is always the first to see her after her ordeal, and she feels a certain affection for him.

Kamala takes her time on the ice cream bar, waiting for the cream to melt off in streams and then coaxing the liquid deftly onto her tongue. She concentrates on the ice cream like a little girl. Soon the crowds disperse and Kamala can move in so that she and the snack seller can have their daily talk.

"So!" Kamala scolds him. "Have you found yourself a wife? A strong healthy man like you, how long can you wait?"

The snack seller smacks an open hand against his shirtless chest and laughs heartily.

"What do I need a wife for? I would only cause the poor thing to shed tears. There's no hurry for me. I will be a good catch all my life."

Kamala smiles wistfully, and watches the man stir the hot oil in which the samosas bob up and down like buoys.

The snack seller smiles bashfully and looks down.

"Anyway," he says softly, "however long I wait, where will I find a woman as loyal as you? Just tell me that. Every man wants the woman of his dreams. Why not? It is no longer a crime to dream, and sometimes...you can never know when...dreams can even come true."

The sunset spreads mauve and bronze over the highrises of Bombay. The waves crash into the sea wall, shooting spray high into the air. The strong wind whips Kamala's sari like a banner and rips apart her carefully plaited hair. The wind pulls on every hair of Kamala's exposed skin as though wrenching them out by the roots. The blood rushes through the layers of her skin as she walks unsteadily toward the sea wall. Her skin is on fire with feeling. Her body burns with a desire of such strength that she has to sit down to keep from falling over. She folds her shaking legs under her and faces the waves. Her skin is like a magnet, attracting wind and light from the air and drops of water from the sea. In these moments Kamala can no longer remember what has come before, so easy is it to sink into the net of vibrating sensation. She can sit with the roaring water for hours in this way.

But sooner or later she burps up samosa heat and the burn of chili sauce bathes the back of her throat once again. The wind dies down and the sunset fades away. In the distance Kamala can hear a B.E.S.T. bus revving its engine.

Kamala reluctantly rises to her feet and looks around. The street is deserted. The office buildings are empty. The snack seller has packed up and gone for the day. She remembers his smiling face again and hears once more the yearning in his voice; the words circle and strengthen around her like a gossamer web: *Every man wants the woman of his dreams. However long I wait, where will I find a woman as loyal as you...*

Younger Wife

The father of Harinath has the most beautiful feet in the world. His big toes are juicy knobs of ginger and his small toes curved cloves of garlic. His soles are as red as chilies, from the mud of the fields where he works. At dinnertime, I jump up when I hear the loud voices of the men returning home. I grab a small pot of water and sit by the door. I wait.

Many men enter our house. They are the blood relatives of my man. Being the youngest wife, I cannot look upon any of them, but I know by their feet who they are. The father of Harinath stops in front of me, breathing hard from the long walk. He stops before me without a word, knowing that in a moment I will take those delicate feet of his one by one into my hands, and wash them carefully by dipping into the bowl and rubbing.

That blessed water is what I wait for all day, to quench my terrible thirst.

First I press my thumb under the toes of his right foot. His toes shiver and shake a little, as though he feels cold. His loud breathing slowly changes, until he is as quiet as a baby sleeping. He has learned how to rest his hand on my head, and he stands as still as a heron on one leg. After I have pressed his foot awhile, I slide my fingers gently between his toes, and his hand jerks and jumps on top of my head with every movement. When I press his toes, he laughs inside with a shaking which nobody else can see. I clean his right foot well, but my impatient hands are already itching to embrace the other.

His left foot is blessed by the gods. Only I know it; everyone else says he is cursed. The father of Harinath has only three toes on his left foot: one big toe, one in the middle and one at the end. In the spaces between the toes are two small knots where the toes can never grow, so small that you can hardly see them. But the father of Harinath can feel them. I rub water on his little toe-buds, as soft as rosebuds, all red from the mud of the fields. I rub and rub till all the dirt is gone. The father of Harinath shakes and shakes with his quiet laughter, and I too, I smile a little inside.

Then he goes inside and I am left at the door with my little pot of water. I touch the water of his feet to my tongue and when I swallow I feel the hunger that hides in my stomach, gripping and squeezing. Sometimes when I stand up my head spins, and I feel like a foolish little girl again.

Harinath is the older of my two sons. The younger one is Somnath. Both boys are healthy and already help their father in the fields. With these two fine sons, life is much better now. But the first one that came sliding out of me was a girl, so my mother-in-law packed my things to send me back to my father's house and told the midwife to bury the girl.

But the father of Harinath said simply, No.

My mother-in-law is afraid that her son with the missing toes will curse the entire family one day, so when the father of Harinath said no, she let me stay, and she let the girl live. The girl works in our house now and is taken care of. We told her she is an orphan, and that she should be happy because we treat her like our own child.

But when Harinath was born, in my heart I knew that this was my real child. When he was a baby, he never cried, because I always knew exactly what he wanted. As he grew up, my son loved me so dearly that the other women in the house were angry. But luckily the father of Harinath has blessed me and my children, and no evil eye has yet hurt us.

Behind my back, my mother-in-law said all kinds of things, that I was a dangerous outsider, that I was turning the father of Harinath against his own family, that I produced one son by some miracle, but that the next one would be a girl-devil. But when the next one was Somnath, a boy bigger and even lighter-skinned than Harinath, I knew that the father of these children, with his missing toes and good heart, was sainted and could never hurt us. No mother should ever doubt the gift of a son, and I feel sorry that my hardhearted mother-in-law has lost love for her own.

This man of mine wants to make more sons. Every night he wakes me up after the children are asleep and quickly does the work to me. Then I think that the chilies rubbed into the soles of his feet have moved through his blood into his essence and from there into the throat of my womb because the flesh tears and burns inside and the tears come to my eyes. Learn to eat chili, the women told me, so that you get used to the burning of your man's work inside you.

Afterwards I turn around and lie down with my face against his left foot, rubbing the warm buds of his missing toes. While he sleeps, the toe-buds jump and shake inside their skin, like flies trapped under a cloth. But after doing the work to me, no matter how much I rub and tickle his toe-buds, my man stays asleep. They are my own special toys, for licking and sucking, like nipples for a baby.

Sometimes, lying there in the dark, my mind wanders and I think of things. I wonder what the good-for-nothing orphan girl is up to at night, wonder which man is feeding her and which one is beating her. Better that a man takes care of her, better than being anybody's helpless child.

My father said I was never a child. I always took care of him, while nobody needed to take care of me. He used to call me "younger wife," because I took my mother's place when she left me alone with him. I would wake up at night and father was always awake, so I would put his head on my shoulder and put my face in his chest and that way we both would fall asleep. He didn't want me to marry, and I grew old in his house until finally, when he was dying, he decided it was time. By then the only man left for me was the one no girl would marry, cursed because of his left foot.

My heartbroken father didn't care whose house I was going to. He stopped talking to me, just like that, and soon after the marriage he died.

He used to tickle me so much! But then he stopped. He would oil and comb my hair every day, but then he stopped. He would feed me my breakfast before he went to work, putting one-one piece of bread and chili in my mouth. He stopped. On the day of my marriage he said that all those things he did to make me happy were because I was his "younger wife." But now I was going to become another man's *proper* wife, the preserver of his household and the mother of his sons, and spoiling me would do no good.

Sometimes when I think about it I feel bad, but I don't know why. I have everything now, more than any woman I know. But my happiness is my secret. No woman would believe me, and none could imagine herself in my place.

I sucked on my mother's breasts till I was six years old. My mother knew that no more children would be coming out of her, so she gave all the milk for her sons to me. I followed her around the house. Wherever she stopped, I stopped there too and sucked on her breast. She was a small woman, and I was not so small. I pushed back her sari and helped myself. Sometimes the breast would jerk and jump out of my mouth. But I always caught it again. It was very sweet.

When Harinath was born, my mother-in-law was finally happy. But one day the father of Harinath said, while watching the boy suckling, the milk is so sweet, just like your milk, isn't it mother? My man's mother ran back, back to the far wall of the room, shaking and trembling.

You were not born of me, said my man's mother. You never tasted the milk from my breasts. You cannot remember it that way. My man laughed, but not the laughing-shaking from inside. Everyone in the village knows I am your son, said my man, even if you don't. Even now, I remember your breasts clearly and can draw them in the sand, those hard sacks of wheat with broken pomegranates on top.

Don't talk about me that way in front of your wife-slave! screamed my man's mother. And in front of your cursed son! My man laughed and made room for himself at my breast, sucking the milk out of me with such force that I could hardly breathe. My mother-in-law covered her face in shame and ran out of the room. I lay back and put our son to one side, and in the broad daylight, in the front room of the house for receiving visitors, he did the man's work in me.

When Somnath was born, my man would wake up at nighttime and feed at the same time as the baby, but on the opposite side. If he tried to do the work to me, I would push the baby between my legs and hold him there tightly. And then from one breast I pressed the milk slowly onto my man's face, swung the breast slowly around until it slid across his forehead from side to side and up and around his nose, until his eyebrows were dripping onto his tightly shut eyes and his eyelashes beaded white.

My man wants to make more sons with me. In the nighttime, he asks the orphan girl to massage his back. She cannot stop until he orders it. I sit there and watch. After a while, he turns onto his back and the girl and I see clearly that it is time for my man to do his work. I know that my man will pull the closest one to him, so I push the orphan girl away and open the throat of my womb for his water. When he sleeps, the girl and I lie down together with our faces at his feet. I have shown her the toe-buds which are my own playthings. She watches me as I drown in their rosy fragrance, sucking on the unborn buds. She lies back for now, too lazy to enjoy a man who makes her work, but from the tightness of her body I know that she too will become a "younger wife" very soon.

Shakuntala

Shakuntala sat in the back, outside the servants' room, shelling peas. The pods were soft and ripe and had light and dark seeds in them. Memsahib had shown her the exact size that the peas had to be. Any peas that were larger or smaller, Shakuntala was to throw away. She picked up a pod, cracked the top under her thumbnail, peeled it down to the bottom and squeezed until the skin burst. The peas flew out and landed in the folds of skirt bunched in her lap. When a handful had collected there, she gathered the bunched material and snapped it hard so that the peas jumped up and landed in the metal bowl caught solidly between her feet.

Two thick silver rings were fastened tightly around her right ankle, and she often scratched at the irritated skin underneath. The rings were carved with a looping design, running deep into the metal. They had been on her foot since she was a young girl. They rang against each other like muffled temple bells.

Shakuntala moved as the sun moved, sitting at the edge of the shade. There she got both light and cooler temperature. She tore the pea pods at eye level, hands outstretched. Sometimes she found small worms and cracked those on her thumbnail as well. Her work was slow and repetitive. After a while her back would stiffen up and her fingers start to fumble, until she began humming a favorite song which helped pick up the pace that set her once more to pressing rapidly on the bulging pods and sending fountains of peas into the air. The peas to throw away she would tuck into her heavy cotton blouse. Occasionally she would find a very large, very green pea which she tucked under her tongue, sucking it with hissing sounds until it softened and melted. Smacking her lips loudly, she would wriggle her body back with the receding shade.

—Shakuntala! Ehh Shakuntala!

—Yes memsahib.

—Go on now, leave the peas alone. Go get those two children and give them a bath. They have to be ready on time.

—Yes memsahib.

—Arrey woman! At least put the peas away. You don't want the birds to eat them. Where are you putting the peas? Put them in the fridge...but cover them first! They'll get as hard as stones. Put them in the green bowl. Look at this mess in the fridge. Didn't you tell the cook to clean the fridge? Damn bastard, who does he think he is, living in my house without doing any work. Just wait, one of these days, I'll finish him off. Nothing but headaches. Now wait...hold the bowl. I have to make room.

—Yes memsahib.

—Where's my radio? Shakuntala! Where's my radio? It was by my bed this morning so you must have seen it. I want to listen to my program. Always disappearing when I need it.

—Yes memsahib.

—Make me some tea, not too much sugar, and wash your hands for god's sake before you touch anything. Look at your fingernails! Your hands are always filthy. And bring the radio from the good-for-nothing cook. He keeps it hidden under his pillow. I swear there's no end to the trouble that man causes here. Listen, don't put any milk in the tea, I have an upset stomach. All this rainwater has filled the tanks with worms, I just know it.

—Yes memsahib.

Working in the desert heat day after day, every woman's blouse stays damp in the armpits. But Shakuntala's dampness stretched from each armpit all the way across her blouse in a run of star-shaped blotches which converged in a thick band reaching down to her navel. She wore the long mirrorwork blouses of her region and a full skirt crowded with embroidery. My mother wore a much shorter blouse, which left a wide band of skin exposed from her ribs to her waist. Her blouses were plain, with no mirrorwork, but lots of stitched darts in the fabric, from the shoulders down and diagonally upwards from the armpits. Because of the darts, even when the blouse was hung from a hanger, the cups of the blouse remained round and pointy, like balloons filled with air.

Shakuntala had too much milk in her breasts. Once or twice a day, she would stand against a wall, leaning against one shoulder for balance, pull up the front flap of her blouse and squeeze the milk out of her breasts in quick jerks forward and downward. Within seconds, hundreds of ants would appear at the base of the wall, scurrying to collect the milk while dodging the continuing bursts of sweet liquid. Shakuntala would groan as if in pain, then suddenly shiver in the burning heat and rest her head against the wall. If she saw me, she always laughed happily and motioned for me to come and squeeze out the remaining milk. I never went to her, but neither did I run away.

—And listen, next time don't let the children play outside without the gatekeeper watching. When he goes for his lunch, bring them back in. Let them do what they want inside the house but they are not to stay outside on their own. I know what kind of good-for-nothings are always passing by the gate. They can play Up-Down or L-O-N-D-O-N or whatever they want inside, but don't let them bring any worms in or there will be holes in the furniture again.

—Yes memsahib.

—Here, come over to this side for a minute and press...wait, I'll open my blouse...higher, no, use your whole hand...yes, yes that's it. Ohh...such pains...that cook is going to make my whole body ache, I swear. Aaah...hmm...your fingers are very rough, but that's okay, don't stop...Mmmm...Now press a little lower...little lower...No, *lower*, it's okay! Aaaah...ohhh...that cook...god only knows why I put up with him...aaaaahh, yes. You can go now.

—Yes memsahib.

—Now listen you, don't tell the cook what I'm doing, and just send him straight to the office room. Tell him to stay there until I arrive. If he starts grumbling, tell him Memsahib might be giving him a raise. Don't listen to his dirty mouth, pretend that your ears are closed or something, knock on the side of your head a little like this, as though you're banging the water out. Arrey, woman, look! Like this, don't beat the top of your head, you don't want your little brain to break into pieces. So lock the office room from the outside and just let him wait in there and we'll see what happens, that dirty robber. He has to understand who is in charge here! You hear?

—Yes memsahib.

—Make sure that he doesn't touch anything or before you know it he'll steal something and stick it in his pants. And that too—his hands are never clean. Lot of good it does to have a brahmin cook who never washes his hands. What all he's up to in the back room, we'll never know. So keep your eye on this thug, just ask him in a friendly way what he is cooking for dinner or something like that and tell him to wait until I get there. If the children are screaming and shouting, just tell them to be quiet and if they don't listen, tell them the devil-cook will chop them into bits for his dinner. That will keep you all busy.

—Yes memsahib.

Finally it was time for the delivery of the entire year's supply of rice and wheat. Bins and bins of grain had to be picked through by the plateful, to remove the small stones which were thrown in to cheat on the weight, and to kill the worms which would eat through every last grain. It was a race against the clock. Shakuntala sat in the back all day long, bent over the platefuls of grain. She worked with great speed, oblivious to everything else around her. In those hectic days, I would come sit next to her. She sat with her back against the wall, the thali resting on her bent knees. Her skirt would be arranged in a dome on the floor around her, her feet hidden from sight. I liked to watch her skirt move about as though by magic. It looked like her feet were kicking the skirt out on one side, or pulling the hem in on the other side, but only I knew that her colorfully embroidered skirt was actually the shell of a tortoise, whose head and feet were tucked under the dome of its beautiful shell. I would sit next to Shakuntala and gently ease my toes under the hem of her skirt, waiting in anticipation for the tortoise to bite my toes.

If I was careful, I could slide my toes, ankles and calves inch by inch under Shakuntala's skirt until my legs were fully stretched under her bent knees, like a railroad tunnel cut through a high hillside. I could sit that way for hours watching her profile, sit that close to her, and she would hardly be aware of my presence as her hands flew across the metal plate, inching a few grains forward at a time, spreading them in a single layer and flicking off the stones, dried grass and worms which formed a ring on the floor around her. Once sorted through, she tipped the plate of grain into a metal bin by her side and started the process all over again.

I dared not move. Once I was in position, I sat as still as a statue, thrilled at being so close to her secret skin without her knowing I was there. I would lie back on the stone floor and feel the heat of her legs on my feet and calves. The hair on my legs would stand up in goose pimples until the roots of the hair hurt as though they had been twisted and knotted.

It usually took Shakuntala three weeks to clean the stocks of grains. By the fourth or fifth day, when the cleaning was going well, Shakuntala would give me quick sidelong glances every now and then and talk to me about whatever she felt like. I could hardly understand what she said, light-headed as I was from my shallow breathing. I let her words drift over me like the tiny gnats that circled round and round in the still air, chasing each other endlessly, never settling on anything.

At night, lying in my bed I would imagine what would happen if Shakuntala were to suddenly roll forward into a squatting position. My legs would snap like twigs, caught between her calves and her thighs, and I would be thrown onto my side. If she were to rock back and forth, I would be rolled from side to side from one hip to the other. Then her strong legs would crunch away on my thin ones, chewing me up like a lizard chews a grasshopper, pulling me down inch by inch until I disappeared completely under her skirt. I stayed awake tense with fear and excitement, imagining the pleasure of the tortoise who could then nibble at me in small bites for as long as it wanted, trapped as I was under the shell-of-skirt.

—Oh god that cook! If you weren't so busy, Shakuntala, I would ask you to fix him once and for all. Torment him, in the way only a loose woman can. He is driving me mad. Work a little faster, no, so you can help me deal with this madman!
—Yes memsahib.
—And look how these children lie around filthy all day because you're too busy to wash them up. When you're all finished with the rice and wheat, take some of that kerosene and rub their scalps because they're sure to get lice. These children just can't keep clean, no matter how hard we work on them. But this one, how quietly she lies down next to you. You've turned her into an angel!
—Yes memsahib.

One more week of cleaning rice and wheat. I decided that Shakuntala knew my secret. I *wanted* her to know. I wanted her to tell the tortoise to come out of its shell and nudge my feet with its wet nose, like a puppy dog. The tortoise must have liked me, to let me burrow into its shell. My body tingled all over as I

approached Shakuntala and sat facing her profile, then inched my
toes under her skirt. She looked at me briefly and smiled
mischievously. My heart leapt, thrilled at her invitation. She has
told the tortoise! I lay back happily and stretched my body taut,
trying to stop the muscles from quivering. I felt the warmth of the
tortoise and explored a little with my big toes. Oh! The furry head
of the tortoise rubbed against my soles. So it was true! I closed my
eyes tightly and concentrated. I waved my toes slowly, like a plant
underwater. The tortoise licked quickly between my toes, once,
twice, then retreated. I couldn't believe it. I opened my eyes and
looked at Shakuntala. She turned to me and winked.

I pushed around with my feet until I felt the soft furry head.
I scooped up its tiny body between my feet, where it rested quietly,
then licked my toes again, this time with long warm strokes. It had
a rough tongue, coarse like a jute sack. It didn't mind sitting still,
occasionally twitching its ears and clawing at my feet with toenails
that tickled.

Shakuntala reached under her skirt to scratch at her ankle rings.
The tortoise quivered in the grip of my feet, straining towards
Shakuntala's hand. I held tight. The tortoise must not escape.
Shakuntala briefly cursed the tight ankle bands, then resumed
picking through the plate of wheat. The tortoise's body then
strained the other way, further in towards Shakuntala's body. I
separated my feet just enough for the animal to spring free. It sat
right up inside her legs, right where she does bathroom. If I listened
carefully, I could hear the tortoise licking. I moved my feet further
in, so that my toes tickled the back of the furry body. The tortoise
turned and licked between my toes again. The tortoise was friend
to both Shakuntala and to me.

Later, I watched Shakuntala from behind a tree, as she made
her way home. That evening her breasts seemed bigger. She would

need to pour out some of the milk. She reached into her blouse many times, as if to press out the milk, but didn't stop by any wall, didn't lean over and press her lovely fountain. Was she all plugged up? Was she falling ill? What would become of her tortoise if she didn't keep in good health?

There was blood on my toes. My mother saw it first. She wanted to know if I had fallen down or if something heavy had fallen on my foot. I couldn't believe it. That tortoise must have bit me! But so gently that I didn't even feel it. So much blood! My mother put my foot in her lap and she looked all over and under the toes, but found no scratch, no bruise, no teeth marks or anything. My mother was furious at Shakuntala. Couldn't the stupid woman keep an eye on me when I was playing around her? My mother wanted to punish Shakuntala, once and for all, maybe even fire her, because she didn't listen properly to the orders given to her. My mother wanted to know exactly what happened. I told her that I couldn't really explain. My mother was ready to lock me up unless I told her what happened, where the blood came from. I told her that I could show her, that I was simply lying down near Shakuntala all day. Maybe the blood fell from a wounded bird? My mother decided to leave the blood on my toes until Shakuntala arrived in the morning, to show her exactly why she was going to be fired. My mother wanted to teach the servants a lesson.

Such problems with these servants, one after another. Hasn't the cook done anything bad to you? Then I can get rid of them both. Why don't you help me, darling, to send him packing once and for all? You are my clever little darling. I'll give you a lovely present if you just make life easier for me.

I knew what I wanted as a present. And I knew how to get it.

—Shakuntala, do you work with your eyes closed? Is it so difficult to look after this precious child who sits respectfully next to you day after day, keeping you company, treating you like a member of the family. Look at her toes. What is the meaning of this blood? Did she hurt herself or did you do something to her? This just goes to show that you are a bad worker and we have no use for your type. You are here only because I've taken pity on you.

—Yes memsahib.

—Now let my baby sit next to you and do what she wants. I want you to take care of her, and make sure nothing happens to her, or you're fired. You and that bastard cook should get together, you're such a crooked pair.

—Yes memsahib.

Shakuntala looked at me in confusion. Her eyes were wide with anger. Why was I getting her into trouble? How would she know where the blood came from? Suddenly she gasped and put her hand under her skirt. I nodded at her. She sucked in her breath in alarm, and crossed her legs tightly. There was a muffled cry from her body.

Shakuntala pushed me away when I sat next to her. She held me away at arm's length. I turned towards the kitchen and looked around, craning my neck this way and that. Shakuntala understood that I was willing to call back my mother, and removed her hand from my waist. She arranged her skirt in a neat circle around her and resumed sorting through the rice. She bent over the plate and worked quickly, trying to ignore me. I lay back and stretched out my body, then wriggled forward until my legs were in position, deep under the shell of the tortoise. The little body of the tortoise immediately sprang forward and I caught the soft furry ball between my feet.

From the corner of her eye, Shakuntala saw me lying next to her. She saw that my feet had disappeared under her skirt. She looked annoyed and glared at me. The tortoise found the blood on my toes and started licking. I could feel a funny tingling racing all the way up my back and into the roots of my hair.

—I know what lives under your skirt.

Shakuntala lifted her palm as if to slap me and I quickly covered my face. Through my fingers I could see one finger on her lips, shushing me.

—I won't tell anyone. I really love your tortoise. But why did it bite my toes and make me bleed? I thought it was giving me little kisses, like it is now.

Shakuntala looked at me in astonishment. She opened her mouth to say something, then stopped and shook her head. Slowly a smile spread over her face, and she sat that way, bent over the grain, grinning mischievously.

—What? Tell me.

She flicked her hand at me, and shook her head again. The smile turned into silent laughter, as she sat shaking from deep within her belly.

—You are like your mother, chasing the wrong animal.

She covered her mouth with her hand and wiped her streaming eyes. She buried her face in her hands, but she couldn't stop laughing. The tortoise felt her shaking, right down to her toes, and strained to escape from between my feet. The plate of rice was rocking on her knees, about to fall over.

—What is wrong with you? I hissed at her.

Shakuntala shook her head and gasped for air, still unable to talk. She motioned for me to wait. She held her stomach and laughed some more, then set the rice down beside her. She signaled me to remove my legs and sit facing her. I let go my precious friend and pulled out my feet. I sat up cross-legged and slid over till I was directly in front of her. I looked at my feet. There was new blood, this time on both feet. I wiped the blood with my finger. It was warm and wet.

Shakuntala looked around to make sure that no one else was about. She rolled up the hem of her skirt, starting at her toes and up over her ankle rings and her knees. Her skin was dark and covered with black hair. She pulled apart her knees, looked around once more to make sure we were alone, then lifted her skirt all the way up to her stomach. Hiding between her legs was a small furry ball of black and brown, the same colors as Shakuntala's skin and hair. Shakuntala reached between her legs and lifted up the animal.

It was a tiny kitten! The kitten licked its mouth over and over, without looking at me. Its eyes were shut.

—The poor thing is blind.

She passed a hand up and down in front of the kitten's eyes.

—Why does it hide under your skirt?

—It is not hiding. It lives there. Only a blind animal will live under a woman's skirt.

Shakuntala spread wide her legs and placed the kitten down in the darkness between her thighs. There were a few drops of blood on the floor and the kitten eagerly lapped up the dark liquid. The kitten moved closer in to Shakuntala, and licked her hairy mound. Shakuntala watched the blind animal licking her and stroked it gently.

—I am feeding her with the only food I can give. Blood and milk.

She reached under her blouse, lifted up the front flap and squeezed a small stream of milk into her cupped palm. She set her palm down on the floor next to the kitten, who turned toward the milk and lapped it out of her hand. Soon a little blood squeezed out from between Shakuntala's legs, and the kitten turned to lick it, then licked the milk from Shakuntala's hand again.

I pushed the kitten away and pushed my finger into Shakuntala's hairy mound. The flesh was soft and wet. Shakuntala slid back at my poking, laughing silently.

—What is in there?

Drops of blood trickled down my palm.

—Why does the kitten bite you and make you bleed? Doesn't it hurt? Shall I bring a bandage?

Shakuntala clucked her tongue in exasperation and rolled her skirt over her knees and down to the floor, covering the hungry kitten in darkness. She wiped her milky hand against her skirt, picked up the plate of rice and resumed her work.

—What can one bandage do for a woman like me? They buried all my daughters at birth—snatched them away from me. They don't know about this one yet. Just let her be.

—Was your daughter born from the cook?

Shakuntala clapped her hands and grinned at me.

—Yes, yes! she chuckled. This is what happens when a poor tribal woman like me rides on top of a brahmin. That is why there are blind cats in this world.

She slept with the cook? She told you that? She has a daughter by him? I don't believe it! That brahmin has made himself an untouchable! He is going to go straight to hell. Even if it is on the word of a no-good tribal woman, he will have to leave the house.

—Shakuntala, eh Shakuntala! Where are you, woman? This time you've had it. My daughter has finally come to her senses, after spending all her time with you. Have you been sleeping with that demon cook? Well, too bad, because he's gone now. I won't stand for any trouble in my house.

—Yes memsahib.

—You people are like animals, you can't control yourself. Such a bad influence on the daughters of the house. Now where is this cat? Eh? Show me. Hiding under your skirt, isn't he? Out with him. How can you keep a dirty animal around when you're cleaning the grain for the household? Have you no shame? Give me that cat. I'll take care of this blind cat. So small, isn't he? Pretty little boy. You're lucky that your kitty is so sweet, otherwise I would throw you out in a minute. The way you people live, this cat could die from germs. I will keep it with me.

Shakuntala quickly wiped the tears from her eyes. She looked up defiantly at us.

—The poor creature is a girl, memsahib, the only daughter I have.

—Don't talk back to me. This little kitty is already like a son to me. See how he bites! Feisty little boy. His name will be Purush, and like his name, he will grow into a man.

My mother lay on her bed, reading a magazine. I sat next to her, watching the kitten sleeping on my mother's stomach. Sometimes the kitty awoke to lick my mother's skin. My mother was ticklish and laughed and squirmed, jostling the kitten about. The little fur ball dug her small claws into my mother's flesh, making her gasp and giggle.

—What a mischievous little boy! He is having such fun with me. I know, I know, he is your present. But I think he really prefers to be with me.

—It's okay. I'll play with kitty after you fall asleep.

As soon as my mother fell asleep, I pulled off my underpants and placed the kitten under my dress. She sniffed around and meowed hungrily.

—Bite me there. Bite me.

She sharpened her claws on the bedspread, rolled up in a ball against the skin of my thighs and fell quietly asleep.

Waxing the Thing

When I first came to Bombay to work in a beauty salon, I didn't understand anything. They told me to wax, so I waxed: legs, arms, underarms, stomachs, foreheads, fingers, toes. It's like a game for me. I cover the skin of the ladies with hot wax, then quickly-quickly take it all off with a cloth, almost before they notice that it's there. It reminds me of my village school, where I used to draw on the wall with chalk, then quickly wipe it off before the teacher found out. For me it's all very strange, what goes on with these rich-rich city ladies, but I mind my own business. I'm just a simple village girl. Everything about the city is strange to me, so what's one thing more?

There I was, minding my own business, when one day this Mrs.
Yusuf, whose legs I was waxing in the private room, asked me if
I would come to her house to wax her *thing*. I was so stupid, I asked
her to her face, "What is this *thing?*"

Now she was already lying there with her sari pulled up to her
stomach, and her legs bent at the knees, and I was trying not to
look at her big white panties that she was shamelessly showing me
through her wide-open legs, when suddenly she stuck one finger
inside of her panties and pulled the material down and showed me
all her hair *there*. I felt so ashamed! All this time, I didn't know that
the ladies wax down there.

This Mrs. Yusuf said, very sweetly, that only young girls like
me are pure enough in the heart to wax it down there. Naturally
she wanted me to go to her house to do this delicate job. In a salon,
anyone can walk into the private room, even when the curtain is
pulled. Some of the other waxing girls told me that they don't do
such type of work. Why shouldn't I? If they want to pay me better
than at the salon, and on top of that, pay for my taxi here and there,
then what do I care?

So I did the work for Mrs. Yusuf, and she told her friends, and
before I knew it I had more work waxing things than arms and legs
and all. All the ladies like me better because I'm not married. They
tell me that marriage will make me rough, like a man, and then I
won't be able to do the delicate job.

All our Indians, you know, are so rough and hairy. The shameless Indian men are always scratching themselves between the legs
because of the Bombay heat, but the ladies don't have to, because
their skin down there is cool and clean. And definitely the smell
is also a little less.

I never knew how many kinds of smells could come out of these
city ladies' things! Even though they wash night and day and

remove every single hair from their bodies, I tell you, some of them smell down there like an armpit. I tell them to put a little baby powder, or maybe even some eau de cologne on the day that I'm coming, otherwise I have to breathe through my mouth so the smell won't drive me crazy. I never used to notice such smells before, but day in and day out putting wax between their legs, I can't help it, my nose has become very nosey.

I'm not so nosey that I ask them questions or anything, but these ladies tell me anyway about why they like to be waxed down there. These thin-thin ladies like Mrs. Nariman and Mrs. Dastur say that it makes them feel clean, because there's no hair for anything to get stuck to down there. Then the gray–hair ladies like Mrs. Patel and Mrs. Loelka say it makes them feel like innocent little girls again, and they even talk with giggly high voices. But worst of all are the lazy fat ones like Mrs. Singh and Mrs. Vaswani, who tell me it's so much better than getting a massage, giving so much more energy to the body, keeping the blood going all day and all night.

Mostly I don't listen to what they say, but one lady, Mrs. D'Souza, told me a very sad story. She said that she was married so many years and her husband never liked to do the man's work in her and so they had no children. Finally she got angry and asked him what was wrong with him and he said that it was all her fault, that the hair on her thing was so rough that it poked like pins right into his skin so he couldn't come near her. Poor man! Since then this lady makes me wax her thing every week, even when I can't find one single hair. The whole time, she lies there saying prayers to Mother Mary. At least these days someone like Mrs. D'Souza can wax. In olden days what must have happened to these poor ladies?

My mother in the village still lives like in olden times. I tried to explain to her that I do waxing to make money, but she just can't understand. She stays in the house all day, covered from head to toe in her cotton sari, so how will she understand? These city ladies are not like that. They understand everything, or how else would they all get rich-rich husbands?

My poor mother—it's so shameful—doesn't even wear panties. And she sits with her legs wide open. All the old women are like that. They're so shameless, they don't even *want* to wear anything down there. Without panties, how can a modern girl control her monthly mess? When my mother was young and she got her monthly bleeding, she just sat in one corner and spread this mud between her legs until it mixed with the blood and became hard, a lid made of clay to close her upside-down, bleeding "pot." When she stood up, the hard clay cut into her skin like a knife. For five days she was like that, sitting in one corner with a pile of mud, playing with herself like a mad girl. After the five days, when she tried to break the mud, the hair from down there would be stuck in it and she would pull the hair right off. How she would scream! My god, you would think it was the end of the world. Why such a big fuss over a few hairs? That's the difference, I tell my mother, between her and the big ladies. If she knew what was good for her, she would have pulled *all* the hair out.

The ladies definitely want all their hair out. They make me check again and again for even one single hair that I missed. It's not so easy, you know, unless I shine a torch on it, and anyway, who says I want to look down there? In the beauty salon they told us, if you're plucking a lady's eyebrows, don't look into her eyes; if you're threading her upper lip, don't look into her mouth; so if I'm waxing the thing I don't look inside there!

Of course it's my job to get all the hair out, but I can't help it, sometimes the hair just won't come out. I try once or twice, but these fussy ladies are never satisfied. For half an hour I have to feel around bit by bit for any leftover hair, and then even if I find it, how can I wax just one hair? So I have to try to pull it out with my fingers, but even that is impossible because by then the skin has become all sensitive and slippery and sliding.

That Mrs. Yusuf, my god, the way she shouts! "I can feel it, I can feel one hair, not there, other side, in the front, no, no, feel properly, grab the skin with one hand and pull with the other, try again, just wipe your fingers if they're sliding, don't think you can rush away without finishing your job," and on and on. What to do? I don't like digging around in there because I know it's where babies and all come from. But I don't grumble because the fussy ladies always give a good tip. Thank god they are not all like that or I would have to spend the whole day waxing and cleaning the thing of just one of them!

Not that they are in any hurry. They can just lie there all day, I tell you. At least I don't have to work at night, because the ladies only like me to wax during the day. I have to finish before the husband comes home, because the man doesn't like his wife to be locked in a room with some outsider.

Sometimes when there is a new lady who wants me to go over to do her waxing, she will ask, "How do I know that you will do a good job? It requires such talent and if you do anything wrong, I'll have to go straight to hospital." So first I give the new lady the names of some other ladies that I work for, so she can call and find out. And then I tell her that I wax my own thing, not just others', so there's no need to worry. All of them, when they hear this, are so shocked! I'm just a poor village girl, so what do I need to wax for? As though you have to be rich to do it! Am I not a woman like them? Can't I be beautiful like them? If my own sister's husband likes it, then won't mine also want it?

I went back to my village for my oldest sister's marriage, and just to teach her how ignorant she is, I took some wax and clean cloths, and I waxed her. What a fuss that stupid girl made! I had to sit on top of her so she wouldn't run away. But then after the wedding, her husband wrote to me that I should come back to the village and wax his wife again, because everyone in the village tells him he's lucky to have such a clean high-class woman. Until I return, my sister is pulling the hair out from down there one by one with her fingers.

Everyone has something that they can wax, so why not me? I only wax myself once in a while. It's not so easy for me. To wax down there, since I can't bend down to see properly, I have to sit on a mirror. Who would think I would ever look at my own thing? Even all those big-big ladies never look at their thing…and me, I've seen so many dozens by now.

"Don't wax it yet, you're not married!" the ladies keep saying. "You're still thin and pure and innocent, and you're not *prepared* like a married woman for what happens down there. You'll start feeling wrong feelings between your legs and then no man will take a chance with you. That's why we don't let our unmarried daughters wax down there." I tell you these ladies think they know everything. I am going to have a love marriage, and have enough money saved so that I can give a good dowry. What husband will say no to that?

The real reason these ladies don't allow their young daughters to wax down there is because then the daughters will want to have love marriages! And then all the life's work for these rich-rich ladies will go to waste, because if Indian girls are allowed to marry whichever man they want, then who will marry the ladies' good-for-nothing sons? They're very clever, these rich ladies. But very stupid also. They force their daughters to be beautiful so they can arrange a match with a rich boy, but in the end they are marrying off their girls to boys who are exactly the same as their fathers, who make this and that excuse and don't touch one finger to their wives who are waxed clean and ready from head to toe.

So every day, there is plenty of business for the beauty salon, giving these ladies manicure, pedicure, facial, waxing, hair cut, massage...And then some simple village girl like me will come along who doesn't know anything and they will cunningly find some way to get her to wax their thing. And when they feel something down there which makes them feel like human beings, then they're happy.

But who wants to listen to what I have to say? So I keep my mouth shut and do my work. When the time comes to get married, I will have saved enough money so my husband can treat me well. Until then, I am living without worries, so what do I care?

Maria

Maria watched me sitting on the toilet, my seven-year-old body half-sunken into the porcelain bowl. She left the bathroom door open and went about her chores. She knew it would be a while before I was done. She had to wash my behind with a tumbler of water, as I couldn't reach around to rinse myself without tipping into the commode.

I sat on the toilet for hours, playing teacher to a classroom of imaginary children. I taught them how to silently explore the bodies of sleeping servants, how to lift up hems and unbutton blouses. I supervised their awkward attempts, making them repeat the actions till they got them right. Finally Maria would show up to wash me, and I squealed as she hurriedly jabbed her fingers into my bum and splashed me with water halfway up my back.

The servants had their own squat toilet in the back of the house, but Maria preferred our "western-style" commodes. When she had to go, she pulled me into the bathroom with her and I loudly announced to anyone listening that I was going to do Number Two and slammed the door shut. Maria sat on the toilet, giggling and grunting. I swung back and forth on the sagging curtain rod, my legs dangling in Maria's face. We sat with the door unlocked, excited by the idea of being discovered, but nobody ever found us out.

Maria slept on the floor next to my bed every night. She slept on a thin mattress without a sheet to cover her body. By morning, the buttons on the front of her dress were often undone, and the hem was hiked up around her hips.

Many nights I cautiously reached into her dress, folding the material back, exposing her cheap nylon bra. The bra covered her loosely, so I could reach under the cup to stroke her breast. But before taking her whole breast into my palm, my movements invariably jostled her and she pushed my hand away.

"Let me," I commanded her, "I'm not going to do anything."

"It tickles," she mumbled, rolling over. I returned to my bed, frustrated by my clumsiness. I shut my eyes and relived the exact sensation of exploring Maria's body, mentally steadying my nervous hands and gracefully covering both her breasts with my adoring fingers.

I heard the front door slam and the key turn in the lock, and I knew that my mother had left. Saturdays were my mother's shopping days. I knew Maria would sneak into the shower.

Normally she bathed out of a bucket in the servants' quarters, squatting down fully clothed, sloshing water over her head with a tumbler, just as she had always done in her village. But slowly she was getting used to the pleasures of our home.

Maria slipped into the bathroom and locked the door. She knew I was aware of her showering every week, but she also knew that I wouldn't tell my mother. Maria was afraid of me, even though she was a grown woman and I was a child. There was never any doubt in my mind about who was in charge.

I heard the shower come on, and the water beating against the tile. I had removed two panes of glass from the bathroom vent which let out onto the balcony. Standing on my chair I could see exactly what I wanted without being seen myself. I stepped up to the gap between the slats of glass and looked down.

Maria was washing her hair, sudsing vigorously. Her eyes were closed. She was humming, and her long nipples were tipped up as she reached around to soap her back.

She rinsed the soap out of her hair, lathered her armpits, and then bent at the knees to rub between her legs. With every motion backwards, her hand disappeared from view.

I was stunned to be looking at her. My legs shook and my head swam so I had to lean forward and rest against the frosted glass. Maria spread her buttocks to let the water in, arching her back, then bending forward. I felt her fingers moving as though they were my own and I suddenly wanted to share with Maria how excited I was.

I giggled, and Maria looked up. She saw my face and screamed. She covered her body with her hands and crouched down until she was bent over on the tiled floor and her breasts and thighs and belly were hidden within the tight embrace of her arms.

She cried and begged, but the water ran into her mouth so her pleas came out as gurgles. One breast swung free as she reached up to turn off the shower tap. She moaned to me to leave her alone, she hadn't done anything, it wasn't fair, she just wanted to finish bathing.

She slipped and lost her balance. She fell back onto her elbows, legs spread wide and breasts bouncing. She scrambled to cover herself back up. I told her she could stay in the shower as long as she wanted, I wasn't going to do anything to her. Maria whimpered and cradled her head on her drawn-up knees. She just sat there. It was over. I stepped down and dragged the chair back into the room. I sank down onto the bed, exhausted.

My mother didn't like Maria very much, because Maria answered back. My mother was irritated by Maria's playfulness, and grumbled that she and I were always up to something. Servants were meant to do work.

Maria came to live in our house when I was born. She was a dark thin woman with a few gray hairs, a wraith who moved around like she was invisible. She was sometimes in the room for many minutes before I noticed her, at which point she stiffened, dodged, cleared her face of any expression, then surrendered herself to being visible.

Maria had children of her own in a village far from Bombay, but since the children were grown up, she claimed that they didn't need to see her anymore.

In the evenings she and I went for a walk along the sea wall across from our apartment building. There we met other women named Anna and Sylvia and Rosie who worked as maids and who also wore dresses. They spoke to each other in Konkani for hours, tightly holding down their dresses which ballooned in the strong sea breeze.

We also had two men working in the house, a cook and a

housecleaner. The cook was a dark puffy-faced, moustachioed man who resembled a bandit. He prepared exquisite food, and was the envy of all my mother's friends. He had never tasted most of what he cooked for us because he was a strict vegetarian. His face revealed only boredom. We didn't know what his real name was. My mother had always christened our cooks "Babu," so that's what we called him.

Ram, the housecleaner, had worked in my father's office for forty years before being transferred to "houseduty." He was a fixture in our house and everyone ignored him but me. He was an older man with long legs that were tight with ropy muscles. He wore very baggy shorts, and I could lie down on the floor while he was cleaning the house and look up his legs. It was all darkness in there, except for his rounded buttocks. The two men slept in the servants' quarters attached to the kitchen.

Every night my mother locked the door of the servants' quarters, so that Babu and Ram couldn't enter the house at night. Every morning at dawn, my mother unlocked the door to let them out. She never entered their room.

The cook fixed the lock so it wasn't really locking. Every few nights, Maria went into the servants' room. She would return before dawn and quickly fall asleep on her mattress. I always heard her come in. She knew that I knew, but also that I wouldn't tell. When I asked her what she did there, she said she helped the servants to fall sleep. I imagined that like little children, Babu and Ram lay down on her outstretched legs and she dandled them on her knees until they drifted into slumber.

Maria didn't say anything about the shower incident. But on Monday morning when it was time to braid my hair for school, she sank the comb into my scalp and jerked it through my knotted hair until I screamed. She shushed me, smiling maliciously. "Sit still," she whispered, "or I'll pull your bloody hair right out."

Every night that week I dreamt of a woman running down the street, tearing off one article of clothing after another—shoes, socks, coat, skirt, blouse, scarf—until she was down to her panties. She could not remove that last bit of cloth. She started again, fully clothed, tears streaming down her face in anger. She ran toward me, removing the clothing bit by bit, looking straight at me with pleading eyes. She came closer and closer, until she finally ran over me. It was terrifying.

I woke up one night with my heart hammering in my chest and I cried out in fear. There was no response, only the whirring of the ceiling fan. I was sick to my stomach. I had to find Maria.

The cockroaches scurried out of sight as I turned on the kitchen light. I walked to the back and pushed on the door to the servants' room. It was unlocked and swung back silently. Behind the door was a small passage that zigzagged around into the dank still chamber where the men slept.

I stood a moment in fear, forgetting why I was there. The air was thick with a pungent odor, an odd mixture of hair oil and urine and sweat. It was the smell of Maria. It was the smell of the cook.

There were two string cots in the room, and as my eyes adjusted to the darkness, I saw the forms of Babu and Ram on the two beds. Maria was nowhere to be seen.

The room was stifling. The men were snoring, deep in sleep. I checked under the beds, then checked behind the door of the squat toilet. Where was she? I would have to wake up the cook to ask him and then he would know that I knew and he would get scared and run away from the job. And then Ram would be suspected as an accomplice, and my mother would have to let him go as well.

Suddenly I heard Maria's long sigh and the cook rolled over

onto his back and there was Maria, her thin body coming up for air. Her dress was unbuttoned, the hem dragged up to her waist. Between her legs I saw a dark patch, and the nightmare came rushing back into my head, about the hole between Maria's legs where the men's heads disappeared when she lay them out on her legs right up against her crotch and dandled them. Inside her hips the heads nestled, and when I poked at her bum the way she poked at mine on the toilet, out came the eyelashes, tongues, ears of Ram and Babu.

The next day I decided. I told Maria I would have her fired unless she did what I wanted. "Baby, don't tell okay, don't tell, baby, okay?" she begged and pleaded. She let me push aside her blouse, unsnap the bra, and push the nylon fabric out of the way, up against her neck, framing her breasts with the twisted, absurdly pointing cups. She bit on her lips and sucked in her breath as I pushed and pulled on her nipples. She tried not to giggle, but no matter how rough I was, she felt ticklish.

When I tried to reach beyond her stomach, Maria writhed and twisted and crossed her thighs tightly. I asked her what she was hiding in there and she gasped, "Same as you, baby, only same as you."

I was unhappy. Maria's nipples told me nothing. The woman in my dreams wouldn't leave me alone. I tried to block her out of my dreams by not sleeping. But she entered my daydreams and leapt around, running down the street helplessly, losing her clothes endlessly. I threatened Maria again. I said I had to see what she was doing with the cook. Maria stuck out her jaw and dared me to tell my mother. She said matter-of-factly that now I was caught; that if I told my mother anything, she could tell my mother something too. Maria would only lose her job, but I had to live with my mother forever.

The sleepless nights exhausted me. I cried and cried at night, but the woman ran down my mind, her footsteps louder and heavier, her clothes clinging to her, suffocating her. She tore them off herself in a hopping-skipping rage, eyes wild with fear.

I had to get into the servants' quarters.

I lay down on Babu's sagging cot, clutching my stomach and groaning. Maria and my mother came running. "Oooohhhh…" I moaned. "My stomach, I can't get up!" I drew my knees into my chest and clung to the edges of the cot.

"What, baba, what is it?" My mother knelt on the floor and tried to feel my stomach. "Don't touch me, don't touch me!" I screamed. "I can't move. Please just let me sleep here."

My mother stiffened with disgust and stood up. "You can't sleep on this filthy mattress. You have your own bed. We'll carry you there and you can sleep till morning. Maria, grab her knees and I'll take her arms."

"Why can't I just sleep here!" I screamed as they picked me up. I thrashed and twisted but couldn't get free. Maria murmured "left, right, left, right" in time to my scissor-kicks, all the way to the room.

"Where do you get these ideas," my mother fumed. "We give you a nice clean house to live in and you want to sleep in the pigsty!"

Three flying cockroaches on the wall, all waiting for Maria. She entered the room and I slammed my fist against the wall. One cockroach flew down and then right up Maria's dress. Maria screamed, threw down the clean laundry and danced around the room in terror. She pulled off her dress and squirmed out of her bra and panties. Out jumped the brown whirly-top, fluttering like a butterfly around Maria's bouncing breasts. She picked up a shoe and swung at the cockroaches, one-two-three, missed them and watched them fly up to the ceiling. She stood with her legs apart, following the cockroaches with her eyes, shoe raised to strike.

There she was, naked and shaking. I walked behind her. The cockroaches paused on the ceiling. Maria concentrated on them with her neck craned back. I lay down on the floor right behind her, and looked up the crack of her legs. The cockroaches didn't move. Maria wasn't aware of me underneath her. Between her legs there was a lot of hair...could have been moustaches or long nose hairs or even somebody's head.

I sat on the floor of the bathroom, my back against the door. Maria sat on the toilet, her dress pulled down around her knees, eyes shut in concentration. "Oh baba," she grunted. "Save me, Mother Mary!" she gasped. I could see it was tough for her, what with all the heads inside. Would she take my help...

"Can I poke you a little bit?" I offered eagerly. Maria swayed back and forth on the toilet. She opened one eye and stared at me. "If you can't clean yourself, how can you clean me?" she asked slowly. "You'll put your finger in the wrong place and my bum will stay shitty."

"What wrong place?" I asked.

Maria squealed with delight. "You think children are born all shitty or what, baba. You think I would touch your bum if that's where babies came from?" Maria hawked up a gob of mucous and spat contemptuously into the basin. "You people grow up in these big-big houses and you don't know which hole is what!"

"Don't shout at me," I cried, utterly confused. "I don't have any other hole. It's not my fault," I said stubbornly. "Only married girls have that other hole."

"You bloody basket," Maria said bitterly, "you can't fool me with your tricks. One is not enough for you, and that's why you're after my hole! You go take your mother's if she doesn't want it. You just leave my thing alone."

I sat naked against the long mirror in my room and looked at what was between my legs. Thin purple skin, folding this way and that. What hole? I touched my navel. I dug into the opening and winced at the pain. The hole was closed. Bloody woman telling me lies, I fumed. I'll fix her once and for all.

I lay in bed listening to the first screams from the servants' quarters. It was still dark outside. The woman running down the center of my mind was slowing down. She could rest for a while, now that Maria would be leaving. I got up, made my bed, put on my school uniform and went into the kitchen.

The cook squatted dejectedly outside the kitchen door, head in his hands. Inside, my mother was at the door to the servants' room, dragging Maria forward with all her strength. My mother's hair was still uncombed from sleeping, falling to her waist. Maria's hair was stiff and matted around her head. They were screaming at each other.

"You get out now, you get out of my house!" my mother shouted, over and over.

"Don't touch me!" Maria screamed, trying to free herself. She saw me and called to me helplessly. "Save me, baba," she cried, "or your mother will kill me."

"Get out, get out, get out," my mother shouted. "You shameless woman, I have a young daughter in the house!"

Maria slammed my mother against the refrigerator and freed

her arms. My mother stumbled, holding the back of her head in pain. I ran up to her. Maria fixed me with eyes of hate.

"Mummy, Mummy," I said, holding onto my mother's waist.

"It's okay, I'm okay," she groaned. "Your father's still asleep; we mustn't disturb him. Call the watchman at the gate. Tell him to come up with the janitor right now. This woman has lost her mind."

"But Mummy, what's happening?" I asked innocently.

"Don't ask questions!" she snapped. "You want this woman to kill us all?" I ran to the intercom, called the watchman and ran back to the kitchen. Maria and my mother stood facing each other, breathing hard.

"All these years, I knew there was something wrong with you. How stupid I was to let you stay!" My mother's voice trembled with anger. "I'm sending you back to your village. You have spoilt my household. Ungrateful woman. You pack your things and get out. And take that son-of-a-bitch cook with you!"

"I don't want him," Maria spat. "He's nothing to me. You keep him to make your mutton fry, cheese toast and what all. He stinks of your food."

My mother covered her face. "You people just won't learn," she cried helplessly. "Such shameless behavior when there's a simple child in the house. Thank god she told me that something was wrong or you would have really twisted her mind."

Maria raised an eyebrow and looked at me sardonically. My heart jumped into my mouth. For a minute she was back to being naughty old Maria, and I smiled hesitantly. But then her lip curled and she snorted in contempt.

"Simple my foot," she sneered, looking me up and down. "Bloody basket, this girl is more shameless than dogs."

"Just listen to her," my mother murmured in disbelief, "who

could tell she is a mother of children herself!"

The doorbell rang. My mother motioned for me to watch Maria and ran to answer the door. "It won't be the same after you're gone," I whispered to Maria. "We always had so much fun." Maria stared at the wall, ignoring me.

The watchman and the janitor, two bent old men in khaki shirts and shorts, entered the kitchen, saluted me limply and walked hesitantly toward Maria. She stepped back, curled her fists and growled. The men looked around helplessly at my mother.

My mother firmly took Maria by the hair, and the two men twisted Maria's arms behind her back and marched her out of the front door. Maria grimaced with the pain of being pushed and pulled, but said nothing. At the lift, the men pushed Maria in and my mother let go her hair. My mother pulled out some money from inside her sari blouse and told the watchman to go with Maria in a taxi to the train station, buy her a one-way ticket to her village and make sure that she was on the train when it pulled out of the station.

"Don't worry," my mother said firmly to Maria, "I'll send every last thing of yours by parcel post." My mother pulled shut the lift door and Maria started crying. "I don't want anything, memsahib," she whimpered, "I just want to stay here with you and baby."

The lift descended, and my mother pulled me to her. She shivered involuntarily. "You just can't trust servants anymore. Just can't trust any of them to take proper care of children."

"But I'm so small," I cried. "Who will take care of me?"

"I know, I know," my mother soothed, stroking my hair. "I'll check in the building and see if anyone knows of another ayah."

"But Mummy, I need somebody today, another Christian girl!" I pleaded.

"Of course, sweetie, I'll find a girl today itself, and this time younger, okay? So you have someone closer to your age to play with."

I smiled at her and jumped up in excitement. "Can I call her Maria?" I asked happily.

"Of course, my darling," said my mother, hugging me and leading me into the house. "You can call her anything you want."

This Anju

These three sons of mine all insist on choosing their own brides. Who am I to say no to them? It's best if they don't involve me in such matters. I'm of a different generation, baba; who can tell which girls are good or bad for them? All I know is who will make a wife and who won't. And this Anju, I can tell you, doesn't know the first thing about being a wife. In all my years I have never met such an aggravating woman! She's put such funny ideas about marriage into *my* Sanjay's head. She thinks she has the answer to everything, but let's just see how long this Miss Know-it-all will stay so bold.

I had nothing to do with this Anju's meeting my Sanjay. I call him *my* Sanjay, because clearly he takes after me. Sanjay is a lovely boy, so talented; he's everybody's darling. He has so many friends, you can't even count them. And on top of that he's just so handsome, like a film star! Right from his school days, so many girls have been running after him, literally hundreds of them. Who can blame them? Naturally, this Anju would feel attracted to him too.

Sanjay is my oldest, and his two younger brothers are complete copycats. But it's just not the same, because they take more after their papa, Dev. Anil and Tarun are very shy with girls, and even with me, their own mother! So naturally I'm concerned about how they will get married, no? Still, if I mention any nice girl, the two younger ones go on and on like parrots about choosing their own girlfriends. It's one thing if you know how to, like Sanjay. Of course, some people call him a Romeo and all, but really they're just jealous.

"How can you let him run around like that? What if he gets some girl into trouble? What about your family name?" They keep asking all this rubbish as though Sanjay is my daughter! God has given me three healthy sons, no, so can't I have some fun in this life?

My Sanjay is an artist, I don't care what people say. There is a reason for the way he is, wandering around Bombay, staying out all night. I never ask where he goes or what he does; why should I meddle? In his college days we heard that he was sleeping with foreign hippie girls in some cockroach-y hotel in Colaba, even paying them money. Why would I believe such stories? Why would Sanjay need to sleep around like that? He had all these girls from good families chasing after him.

Not that a traditional girl would have done for this mad boy of ours! His head is full of jazz-shazz and he's all the time playing drums in the air and singing pa-pa-pa-pa-dhish-dhish and there's that ring in the top of his ear and he doesn't wear any underwear and god knows what all he's been smoking all these years. In a way he must have been lonely, because of course the girls of Sanjay's age all got married right after college. So when he met Anju, at first I was very happy that at least she was a decent girl of good family. The only reason she was single was because she had been studying all these years in the States. At least, that's what I thought until I got to know her better. Sometimes I think she must be just pretending to be Indian, an impostor. I realize that she's become Americanized after all the years away, but then she should at least talk like one, or dye her hair blond or wear some funny clothes, so that we can all see clearly that she is one of them and not one of us.

The truth is, I have always wanted to know everything about my Sanjay's life, but you know how it is, after they get older, children like to keep their secrets. So I arranged this special plan: every time Sanjay needed money, he would come to me, and no matter how much he asked for, I gave it to him, as long as he told me honestly what it was for. In this way I learned about all kinds of new things, like discos and cocaine and jam sessions and big-big parties and sometimes he told me about girls he wanted to buy little gifts for. In my humdrum life, it was nice to hear of such excitement from my son.

That was how I first heard about this Anju. She had asked Sanjay to buy a small Walkman-type recording machine, so the two of them could carry it everywhere and talk. I remember thinking to myself, this is very odd. What is she up to? Is she going to blackmail my Sanjay? Maybe he shouldn't say anything into a recording machine. What if something happens? Dev would never forgive me. I kept asking Sanjay to bring her to the house, and he said, "I will, I will," but weeks went by and there was no sign of her.

I asked Sanjay to tell me a little bit, what he likes about her and so on. He told me, "She knows me so well, it's as though she can read my mind. She is so honest; I've never met anyone like her." And to prove it, he showed me some letters she had written to him. Horrible things! Terrible, thick letters, full of millions of words all pointing to Sanjay saying *You you you!* Poor fellow. I mean, why did she have to write such letters where everything was spelled out in detail? Why not just say a few words in private?

My poor son. He was excited to share with me. I read one page of one letter and let me tell you I got very scared. I thought to myself, Oh baba, I can't read this hot knife of a letter that she is sticking inside my Sanjay, twisting it this way and that. She wrote the letters so that all their problems were out in the open where they could be looked at. *But everybody else can look at them too, no?* Shameless girl, listing all his faults like a shopping list.

I tell you, the *nerve* of the girl! When she finally came to the house, I was so upset, I barely said a word. But she, upstart, she talked the whole time! She said she had come to me for help. She said that Sanjay had some problems with trusting women. Imagine! And did she stop to ask then how he managed to trust his mother? On and on she went: How could she get Sanjay to trust in her? Couldn't I possibly help her? Yakety-yakety-yak.

Did she really think I could take sides against my son? Could I really teach him to trust a woman who is nothing like his mother? Even Dev knows I can never go against my boys. But what to do, I talked to her a little bit. I told her all the usual things a mother can say: men are different; it is a woman's duty to take care of her man; with a little compromise, a woman can find the strength to make things work.

But it wasn't my advice that she wanted, oh no. She wanted me to *talk* to Sanjay. She wanted me to answer some of his questions about *me*, his mother. That was her plan to get him to trust her. In this way, the blame was to be shifted to me! I felt like vomiting, just exactly. What could I possibly say to Sanjay? Not even one word.

I tell you, I felt blamed by her. I just couldn't relax with her in the room. She came during lunch, and I swear I lost my appetite. Halfway through her speech, I just stopped listening and sang songs in my head. I held my breath till my ears started ringing, and then I truly couldn't hear a single word she was saying. *I, me, want, I, me, want.* I swear, she knew only those three words! I got fed up. I thought, my god, Sanjay is involved with a lunatic.

What is this thing all the time of doing what you want and being what you want and finding yourself and losing yourself? There's no right person or wrong person, you know, there's only right attitude and wrong attitude. These Indian girls, they go to America and come back absolutely brainless. They think they know everything. They think they can understand everything. As though such a thing is possible.

Sanjay's daddy, Dev, was the first to say out loud that she's not very friendly, that she doesn't stop for chitchat. There's nothing wrong, I mean, some people just are that way. But once, just for the sake of asking, I asked Sanjay if she was angry at us or what. After all how much effort can it take to say a simple "Hello auntie, hello uncle." But Sanjay didn't like my asking, and he said, "Ma, come on, she always greets you. Don't dig where there are no crabs. She's not like you. When she has something to say, she says it."

They say modern girls are like that, a little on the cold side.

I tried, you know, I tried to be friendly. I told this Anju that sometimes my Sanjay gets nervous and it's very difficult for anyone to take care of him. The things he does! All day without food, only lemon water. Taking one-one puffs from cigarettes then throwing them out. Running up and down the hill till his feet are bleeding.

Talking, talking, talking with somebody, anybody. It's like a fit comes over him. In front of the whole world he punishes himself, in front of the whole world he asks forgiveness, like a beggar-sadhu. It breaks my heart. I can't bear it, baba, to see him suffering this way, but nothing helps him in these moods.

In this way I thought I might scare her a little bit, but right from the start, Anju handled him. When he got into these funny moods, straightaway she would start lecturing him, la-la-la-la-la, for hours. I've never seen any woman so cold! She was like ice, that girl. She spent hours and hours discussing with him. From outside the door I could only hear Sanjay sobbing pitifully, god, it broke my heart when he was that way, and her half-angry, half-laughing voice, asking him why, why he's always hurting himself, and herself... all this-self and that-self. I know for a fact that Sanjay's problems are neverending. He's always been that way. But she knew how to wear him down, till his nervousness was all sucked out of him, till he was completely defeated, with not a word left to say. Anju, cool as a cucumber, would end by telling Sanjay that he could easily fix his life...if he wanted.

As though Sanjay doesn't want to be happy! As though any of us chooses to be unhappy! Why would she talk that way if she really loved my Sanjay?

In this way the time passed. Everything would go well for days or even weeks, until Sanjay had another breakdown. Then he would lock himself in his room, and if I tried to talk to him, he would scream and shout for me to leave him alone. As though it was my fault! Sooner or later, Anju would come, and the two of them would disappear for hours. He would come back looking like all the blood had been sucked out of him. And she would be looking all happy and satisfied.

I told Dev, "These two have some funny relationship, baba!"

It was clear that she was manipulating him somehow, because *he* was always crying, and *she* was always scolding. You check with any woman, and it's always the opposite, like with Dev and me. No matter how many tantrums my Sanjay had, that girl always stayed by his side. Long after my ears closed up from the anger and shouting and cursing that flew out of his body, she stood by him, talking, talking, talking. Nothing scared her, nothing made her go away.

The two of them started spending all their time together. They were inseparable. I thought to myself, be honest and admit that Anju is the be-all and end-all of Sanjay's life. They might get married, and you'll have her as your daughter-in-law! Then what? Better get to know her before she takes over your life.

So I observed this Anju seriously for some time. Quite a lovely girl, very attractive, laughing and joking all the time, and of course her family name speaks for itself. Very clever, with her M.A. from America and all that, and good with money. But in some ways, just like a man. Never wearing a sari, no makeup, no jewelry except earrings, sitting with her legs wide open, taking drinks, talking all big-big talk. Not for one second will she discuss the price of fruits and vegetables or those new actresses on my favorite TV program. Not even a flicker of interest in going with me to the vault to see what jewelry I have set aside for Sanjay's wife-to-be.

All that I could have lived with, but the worst thing was the way Sanjay's two copycat brothers became exactly like her pets, like her stupid faithful puppy dogs. They wouldn't hear a word against her. I tell you, when all three sons stick together like thieves, it's impossible to knock any sense into them. Any chance I had of convincing Anju that Sanjay was wrong for her was completely destroyed once those two younger boys started meddling, waiting on her hand and foot, buying her flowers and what all other junk.

That was the end of that! This Anju was thrilled at having her own fan club, and the four of them became inseparable. So much attention cannot be good for a woman, and sure enough, this Anju turned all my sons against me.

She has never tried to understand me. For all her babble about knowing and understanding and this-ing and that-ing, she was too selfish, really, to waste time on anyone but her Sanjay. I mean, Sanjay was put on this earth by his mother and father. She said, "When I marry, I will be marrying only my one man, not his entire family." The cheek of her! Thank god I only have sons, baba. I don't think I could survive having an unfeeling daughter like her.

I tell you, I got so tired of her meddling and fiddling, so fed up with her coming and going that every time she came near me I got a splitting headache. Why should I have to suffer like this in my own home? So I told Sanjay to stop bringing her to the house; I would welcome her back to my house when she became humble enough to marry my son, devoted enough to be my daughter-in-law, and genius enough to shut her mouth forever.

So now she's left. Just as suddenly as she came, she's gone away. After spending all that time with Sanjay, spoiling and pampering him, turning him into *her* Sanjay, she's left. Two years of putting up with her strange behavior, and just when I am hoping that I can return to having a peaceful relationship with my Sanjay again, he turns around and blames *me* for having ruined his relationship with her! The things he said, I thought I had died and gone to hell. The words are sticking in my throat. He called me a miser, a liar, a coward, a traitor. He said that I have such a jealous nature that Anju was afraid of marrying into the family. He said that...oh dear god, he said that if only he were a motherless orphan, then everything would have turned out fine. That's just exactly what he said. A *motherless orphan*...

What could I say? I just wanted to run to my room and cry. But
he stood there waiting for an answer! I told him that this Anju had
turned his head completely around so that now he was talking to
me in exactly that horrible *you-you-you* way that she always talked.
He said, "Your problem is you just cannot tolerate honesty. She's
put my head on straight, and for the first time in my life, I have
the courage to ask you who you are and what you want. I need
to clear up our relationship. Can you handle that?" he shouted.
"Can you do that for me?" I covered my ears, baba, I couldn't listen
to her voice coming out of my Sanjay's mouth. I said, "You cannot
force me to do such things, I am your *mother!*" And he said, "All
right my mother, I can't live in the same house as you anymore.
Consider me dead." And he left.

And then would you believe *more* trouble? I was cleaning out
the desk of Sanjay's younger brother and I found pictures of this
Anju. At first I thought, how sweet, Anil is keeping them as a
memento, but then I thought, why aren't these in frames on *top* of
his desk, why hidden away? When I asked Anil, he was so angry
with me, so angry, I can't tell you. He said that I had no right to
be fiddling with his personal possessions, he said that if he ever
met a girl he liked, he would never bring her to the house to meet
his jealous mother, he said that he was sick to death of me and was
moving out of the house.

So now, can you believe it, *two* of my sons hate me! What kind
of crazy world do we live in? At least my youngest son is still with
me. But the truth is that he doesn't talk very much, so god knows
what is going on inside his head. Dev says it's all my fault, that
I've always tried to control our boys and make them feel sorry for
me. I don't know what to think. Of course I'm lonely and of course
I want my sons to love me, but how can that be a fault?

What is a mother to do, I ask you.

My own sons, behaving like this with me!

Ohhhh...I tell you, my heart is completely broken. I can't make head or tail of it.

There's a curse on this house, and it's all because of this Anju.

So many weeks alone in the house, without my two big boys. Yesterday I spent the whole day writing letters. I wrote a long letter to Sanjay, who is living in that cockroach-y hotel in Colaba, poor boy. He refuses to come home; he says he wants space. Space! In that filthy broken-down hotel? He's living like a beggar. I also wrote a long letter to Anil, who at least has rented a room at the Club, where they change the bed sheets every day. I wrote them both long stories of their childhood, about how they used to love me like crazy, how they always cried for me when I went away from home, how they wouldn't fall asleep unless they were lying right next to me. I reminded them both about their duty toward their younger brother, who was still impressionable, and to their old mother, who was still waiting for her sons to bring happiness into her life.

That was yesterday.

Today I'm writing a different letter, a kind of letter I have never written before and will never, god willing, write again. Every five minutes I feel like crying, so I stop, otherwise the tears will make the ink run.

I'm writing a long letter to Anju, begging her to come back and marry my Sanjay. I am telling her that I just cannot bear to be separated from my sons like this, that nothing is worth this kind of pain. I am assuring her that Sanjay and I are alike, so if he can stand to talk to her and cry in her arms and be happy with her, then maybe I can learn a little of the same. I'm telling her that Anil will be a devoted brother-in-law and will soon find the courage to find a decent girl to take his name. And I'm crying to her to forget my meddling, that I'm a confused old woman who wants only to see her sons settled and happy.

And lastly, I am buying that recording machine she always wanted, small enough to carry in her purse. She and Sanjay can spend their whole lives filling up cassettes with their misery, the way other people fill up albums with smiling photographs. And then when they're old and all their precious cassettes are broken and useless, then perhaps they will bend a little and open their hearts and allow my old voice to join in with their own.

Just Between Indians

"I wouldn't go in there if I were you," Sahil warned softly. He was dressed in white linen pants and a dark silk shirt, comfortably sprawled on the couch of green and yellow brocade. His eyes sloped down at the corners, adding to his relaxed look. Daya was instantly irritated by his tone. She stopped by the closed kitchen door and looked around the room as though searching out the person he might be addressing. She then turned to look at him.

"Are you talking to me?" she asked with mock surprise. "I just wanted something to drink."

"My father's on the phone with your parents. We could be part

of the same family soon. You wouldn't want to jeopardize it."
Sahil's eyes were twinkling. Daya looked at him as though seeing
him for the first time. He was about five foot, seven in his early-
to–mid–twenties. He looked quite at ease and wore a studied expression of amusement.

"Could you stop smirking long enough to explain yourself?"
Sahil sat up and smiled cheerfully.

"There's nothing to explain, really. My brother took one look
at you and decided you'd do. He's looking for a wife."

Daya had arrived on the airport shuttle over an hour earlier.
She was on spring break from a hard junior year in college, and
had come to New York to explore the city. It was her first visit as
an adult to the home of her father's old friend Rohit Patel. Rohit
Uncle had insisted that Daya stay at his house when he found out
that she was coming East. She would have preferred any place
other than the home of conservative Indian immigrants, but her
parents had pressured her, saying that Rohit owed them a favor,
and in any case, she didn't have the money for a hotel.

When she'd arrived, her fears were confirmed. Rohit greeted
Daya in his megaphone voice and thumped her painfully on the
shoulder, rubbing his palm up and down her back until she
shrugged him off. Daya asked if Veena, Rohit's wife, was still at
work. Rohit informed her, "No, Daya, Auntie Veena is away in
India for a few more days." Daya's heart sank. She couldn't believe
her bad luck. Veena, a big boisterous woman, was as full of humor
and affection as her husband was full of bullying censure. Daya had
been hoping for Veena's laughing presence; instead, Rohit was
playing host to some relatives from London: his widowed brother
Subhash, and Subhash's two grown sons, Ranjan and Sahil.

Daya stood in the front room of the house paralyzed with dismay. One by one the men came up to her. Sahil shook her hand firmly and regarded her with interest. Ranjan offered an awkward wave and stepped back hastily. Subhash patted her on the head like a child. Rohit beamed through the introductions, his hand once again vigorously massaging Daya's back. Finally he let go and Daya rushed up the stairs to her assigned room. Rohit's voice boomed behind her.

"The last time I saw you, you were an ugly duckling! Lucky for you, you've changed."

Daya cursed herself for listening to her parents. She was incensed at the prospect of spending a whole week with this gang of Indian men. *I might as well get back on the plane for home.* She emptied her duffel bag onto the bed and tossed her clothes into the chest of drawers. She kicked the bag under the bed and threw herself onto the mattress. With a wry smile she remembered her mother's goodbye at the airport.

"Learn to relax around people. You get so bad-tempered sometimes. What will Rohit Uncle think if you're badly behaved? Just smile, be friendly and make the most of it. It's not asking a lot; after all, this is just between Indians."

In high school, Daya had denounced her ties to Indian men. She resolved to stay away from them completely. Growing up, she had idolized her two older brothers. As children, the three of them had been inseparable. But as the boys entered high school, one behind the other, they turned against their adoring sister, labeling her "just a stupid girl." The summer she turned fourteen, she begged her brothers to let her join them on a camping trip with four of their Indian friends. After much tearful pleading on her part, they finally agreed, and Daya was elated. They would be going far into the woods, miles away from anywhere. Daya imagined a real adventure in the wild.

The camping trip turned out to be a nightmare. For four of the longest days of her young life, Daya was teased mercilessly. The boys were obsessed with flicking up her dress and shouting "Peep show! Peep show!" To add to the fun, Kishore would hold his sister tightly against him and tickle her, while Krishna reached down her back to snap her bra. Daya returned home, humiliated. She refused to speak to anyone about what had happened. Her brothers tried to joke with her and cheer her up when they saw how withdrawn she had become, but Daya refused to be comforted, and smoldered behind a wall of silence. The following week, the parents of her brothers' friends sent inquiries about Daya's future availability for marriage. Daya was horrified. She went wild with rage. Her parents tried to calm her with assurances that, naturally, marriage was out of the question until Daya reached eighteen. But it was clear to Daya that her mother's assurances only thinly disguised her delight at having received these early proposals.

From then on, in her own house, Daya felt afraid. She knew it was only a matter of time before she would be betrayed.

Sahil stood up as Daya flushed with anger.

"So your dad's on the phone with my parents. Does he think I'm for sale?" she demanded. "We've never even met before!"

She turned toward the kitchen.

"Wait!" He darted after her, but it was too late. Daya jerked open the kitchen door and marched in. She looked around. The phone was resting in its cradle. Ranjan and Subhash were seated at a sunny table at the far corner of the spacious kitchen, eating sandwiches. Father and son looked up and smiled as Daya cautiously crossed the length of the kitchen.

"Can we offer you a snack?" asked Ranjan in his soft English accent. He held up a plate of sandwiches for her inspection. "Dinner won't be served until much later."

"Uh...no. Actually, I...I wanted something to drink," stammered Daya, and wrenched open the refrigerator door. She stood there gasping, the waves of cold air chilling her to the bone. Her mind raced furiously, trying to make sense of the situation.

She slammed shut the refrigerator door and walked over to the table.

Ranjan pulled out a chair for her at the table and grimaced. "I know, there's nothing worth drinking in the fridge. I've told Uncle to buy juice or something..."

Daya sat down, pulled her chair forward and leaned her elbows on the table. "Did I hear you talking to my parents a little while ago?"

Ranjan blushed and cleared his throat.

"I didn't realize we were speaking that loudly...," he began.

"Well, thanks for taking the initiative and informing them that I've arrived safely." She paused, waiting for Ranjan's reply. Ranjan nibbled at his sandwich and said nothing. Subhash gently pushed his chair back, excused himself and went to wash his plate in the sink.

"I mean, that is what you told them, right?" Daya continued. She rubbed her sweating palms against her thighs. "You were making sure that my parents wouldn't worry about me, *right?*"

Ranjan winced at her loud voice and nodded vigorously. "Oh yes, of course. Absolutely! And...and...they send all their love, and they'll call you later tonight when the rates are lower."

"And did they pass on any messages from my *boyfriend?*" she barked.

Ranjan shook his head. "Oh no. Not at all. Perhaps later, when they talk to you in person?" He grabbed another sandwich and sank his teeth into it. The kitchen door swung shut as Subhash exited.

Daya exhaled loudly, feeling the blood pounding in her throat. She looked out over the garden to steady herself a little. The neat lawn reminded her of her parents' yard. Her family was all together for the week; all, that is, except Daya. Right at that moment, they were probably lounging around in deck chairs, playing endless rounds of cards. Her brothers would be mercilessly teasing their pretty new wives and her parents would be attempting to join in the fun.

Daya had disliked her sisters-in-law on sight. They resembled human sponges, ready to absorb all their husbands' demands as well as the commands of their mother-in-law. The weddings were agony for Daya, as she was continually scrutinized and remarked on as an "eligible girl." And immediately after marriage, her new sisters-in-law turned their attention to rectifying the unmarried plight of their dear Daya.

Within months, Daya cut off all contact with her brothers and made sure her visits home never coincided with theirs.

Ranjan darted uneasy glances at her. She turned to him in exasperation. He had a high forehead and curly black hair, high cheekbones and a straight nose. He looked anywhere from twenty-five to thirty years old.

"Your brother tells me you want to marry. Why?" demanded Daya. "Why don't you just pay a prostitute?"

Ranjan stared unhappily at his empty plate.

"That's cruel," he replied softly. "I was actually engaged for quite a while. I loved her. But...she changed her mind. Terrible mess, actually. So I'm...I'm forced to look again."

Ranjan gave a quick pained smile, then once again pushed the plate of sandwiches toward Daya. "Won't you have one? They're quite good."

Daya picked up a sandwich and lifted the top slice of bread. There were slices of cucumber and tomato and a thick layer of butter. *Uptight vegetarians.* "What are you guys doing here in New York?"

"Dad's thinking of moving to New York, so we've all come for a look-see."

Daya gave a short laugh. "You men go everywhere together?"

Ranjan smiled. "You've heard of a two-in-one? Well, we're a...a *three*-in-one." Ranjan waited for Daya to smile at his joke, but she just stared at him.

"It's a joke...," he offered lamely.

Daya grimaced and wiped her mouth. "I have just one thing to say. I won't have you doing things behind my back, okay? If you have anything to say to my parents, you better tell me first. Got that?"

She stood up to leave but Ranjan lifted his hand to stop her.

"So...so...are you here on holiday?" he stuttered. "Because I am too. Maybe we could go do...see...eat something together? My treat of course!" Ranjan ended in a rush.

Daya giggled at the thought of going out to dinner with Ranjan. Ranjan took her laughter as assent and relaxed somewhat. He quickly wiped the sweat from his forehead.

"I know you eat meat and fish," he continued quickly, "and I don't mind. We could go to the Victoria Palace. Have you been there? It's very fancy, you'll be impressed...er...I mean, you'll really like it. I hope you don't mind terribly but I've already booked us a table there for lunch tomorrow since reservations are so hard to come by..."

"You what!" Daya gasped. "How dare you, you...," she stopped herself and stood up, then backed away, with one final warning. "Keep your distance, okay, and we'll get along fine."

"So my brother's incompetent with women. So what's new? Come to think of it, most men are." Sahil philosophized in his best BBC accent. He was reclining on the couch once more. Daya was on her way back upstairs, but she stopped, turned, took a deep breath and approached the couch.

"Well since you seem to know so much, professor, why don't you try to educate him a bit?"

Sahil spread his hands. "I'm here, aren't I? I'm watching out for him. What more can a brother do?" he laughed. "Ranjan really does believe that Dad can get him any woman he wants. And the trouble is, Dad believes it too!" He grinned from ear to ear and snapped his fingers. "It's a ma-ma-ma-ma *man's world* out there!"

Daya felt a smile trying to escape her lips. "That's not funny. I would never have come here had I known that this house was a pick-up joint for Indian men. This is supposed to be my vacation. I should get out of here."

Yet even as she voiced her desire, Daya knew she couldn't leave. Her parents would be furious and certainly refuse to pay a hotel bill.

"If you'd rather stay somewhere else," offered Sahil, "I have many friends in New York. Women. I'm sure they would understand the situation perfectly. None of them are *Indian*, as you might guess."

Daya couldn't help smiling at this last comment.

"Ah," said Sahil with delight. "You're beginning to trust me. Your face really lights up when you smile. I can read you like a book."

Daya clenched her fists in renewed irritation. "Would you please quit with the personal comments? It's really insulting to be checked out like a slab of meat."

"Oh, please! Now you're confusing me with my sexually repressed brother! You'll know jolly well when I'm 'checking you out.'" Sahil bounced off the couch and turned to face the French windows that overlooked the garden.

Daya was astonished at his outburst. What a joke! Each Patel with a bigger ego than the other.

Sahil turned to Daya with a sheepish smile. "I'm sorry, that was out of turn. I'm being insensitive and making a bigger mess of all of this..."

"It's a friggin circus," Daya jeered.

Sahil nodded solemnly and launched into another apology. "I'm sorry, it appears that everyone here is rather worked up. All it takes is for one attractive Indian woman to walk in the door and the next thing you know..."

Ranjan peered around the kitchen door, then stepped cautiously into the living room. Daya moved away in disgust. Sahil quickly stepped in front of her and motioned for his brother to back off. Ranjan's face crumpled in confusion.

"Let's get out of here," Daya whispered loudly to Sahil, "before Romeo whips out the engagement ring."

Sahil tried to keep up with Daya as she walked furiously around the block.

"So, you and your brother have nothing in common."

"Not a thing."

"You have the same parents, you've lived together all your lives and yet you're utterly unconnected."

"Exactly. Those who know us well wonder what in god's name

we're doing in the same family."

"Well?"

"Frankly, I've learned a lot by hanging around with my graceless brother. He makes the mistakes and I clean up after him. It works out well."

Daya puzzled over Sahil's words. *He's pulling my leg.*

"You think I'm joking," Sahil said, "Ranjan really is my lucky charm. In cleaning up after him, I've done my most interesting work and met the most interesting people. Like you."

"Oh I get it!" she cried. "You and your brother do a Jekyll and Hyde routine where he humiliates women and you step in to comfort the poor victims. Right?"

"You've got quite the talent for sarcasm."

"Why did you tell me, anyway? This whole business of your brother looking for a wife. He's such a klutz that I might never have found out, never have gotten insulted, and enjoyed my spring break after all."

"Well, frankly, I like you and couldn't bear to see my brother treat you like some senseless object."

Daya slowed her pace to take in his unexpected words.

"You're *not* by any chance interested in him, are you?" Sahil asked cautiously.

She looked at him in horror. "Are you kidding? No way! Your brother is petrified; I can barely see his face under all that angst. He hates himself. He'd be terrible in bed. I could never be attracted to a man like that."

"I see," Sahil nodded solemnly. "So you *are* as experienced as you look."

"Yes, and not with *Indian* men, either. They could drive a woman to her grave."

Sahil frowned at Daya's words, struggling with some

remembered pain. "I...uh...I wouldn't *exactly* call myself 'Indian.' We were raised everywhere: Africa, Australia, Singapore, Canada, England...I've set foot on every continent."

"I'd rather be dead than involve myself with an Indian man!" Daya continued as though she hadn't heard him.

Sahil frowned again and walked in silence for a while. He resumed in an uncertain tone. "Funny you should mention graves, or perhaps you already knew? It's my mother's death anniversary tomorrow. That's probably why Ranjan is acting like such an arsehole. It's the same every year; he turns into a complete wreck."

Daya flushed with shock and came to a stop. "No, of course I didn't know. How could I know? I don't know anything about your family. We've never even met before. And tomorrow's her...oh god! Is that why your brother wants me to go for...?" Daya stopped herself from finishing the question.

"What?" asked Sahil.

"No, nothing. Never mind."

They walked around the block once again, past the sprawling suburban mansions. Daya looked at Sahil from the corner of her eye. He was just taller than her. His body was stocky, and from what she could see, his chest was covered with curly black hair. He walked gracefully and confidently with his shoulders thrown back. Daya suddenly realized that the Indian men she knew walked very differently, with stiff jerky strides, slouched over or with their chests and stomachs bouncing. He turned to her and smiled.

"You keep looking at me. Do I remind you of someone?" he asked.

Daya shook her head vigorously and exclaimed, "No, I would say definitely not!"

Amused, he looked at her with a warm expression. He looked directly into her eyes and she found herself imagining that she could forget he was Indian.

"Is your boyfriend American?"

"Am I required to answer that?"

Sahil walked in silence for a moment, then sighed. "I was just wondering. I can frequently predict all sorts of things about Indian women. I've, sort of, been observing them all my life. It's a sort of...*hobby* of mine, a bit like solving complex puzzles."

"So *you* must have an Indian girlfriend."

"No, actually. Never have," he replied matter-of-factly. "But there's always hope, don't you think?"

Daya stared at Sahil, stared right through him. *Never had one. He's like me.* She felt a sudden tightness in her chest and closed her eyes. She reached back and pressed her neck. Immediately Sahil moved behind her and she felt his warm fingers on her shoulder, pressing down on the knots of tension.

"What's wrong?" he asked gently. "Are you tired? Would you like to sit down?" Sahil walked around to face her, and Daya opened her eyes. Daya noticed Sahil's eyes clearly for the first time. They were amber, like cats' eyes, covered by thick curled lashes. His gaze was steady, quizzical, concerned.

She shivered. Her teeth were suddenly chattering in the cool evening breeze. She stepped back and hugged herself. "You can't disguise the way you look," she laughed. "You're definitely Indian."

Sahil inclined his head and gave a low bow. "I will take that as a challenge. I shall do my very best to prove you wrong."

"Daya, what can I offer you? We have Coke and other soft drinks in the fridge, or perhaps you'll take tea or coffee?"

Rohit was playing the genial host, bounding around the kitchen, setting out the Tandoori restaurant food he had brought home. Daya and Sahil sat next to each other at the table, with Ranjan across from them. Subhash sat at the foot of the table, and Rohit's place was, of course, at the head.

"Uh...actually, I'd like a drink please. Gin and tonic, if you have it."

Rohit opened his eyes wide in mock alarm and wagged his finger at Daya.

"You naughty girl! You're lucky that Auntie Veena is away because she would be very angry right now. A proper young lady like you shouldn't drink. Lucky for you, I am broad-minded. But keep in mind that liquor is expensive."

Rohit opened the liquor cabinet and pulled out the bottle of gin. Daya silently mimicked Rohit's wagging finger and shook it around the table. Ranjan blushed and looked down at his plate. Subhash cleared his throat loudly and adjusted the napkin in his lap. Sahil looked pointedly at the ceiling. Rohit placed the gin and tonic in front of Daya. All the men were drinking water.

"So tell me," Rohit snickered as he sat down, "does alcohol make you tipsy?" Rohit turned to Ranjan with a broad smile and winked at him.

Daya felt the anger rising in her throat, and was just opening her mouth for a quick retort when she felt Sahil's cautioning hand on her elbow. She exhaled slowly and pressed her lips shut.

Rohit leaned forward with a leer. "Drink up, drink up!" he boomed. "We are all waiting for you!"

"Shall we get started?" Sahil interrupted politely. He lifted the pan of curried peas and potatoes and ladled some onto his plate and Daya's. Subhash took the pan next and looked at Daya as she sipped her drink.

"So, young lady, are you thinking about marriage? I'm sure your parents have received many offers."

Rohit grunted with pleasure as he chewed a mouthful of chapati. "It's essential for our boys to meet girls from good families." Rohit wagged his finger again. "It will help them get sensible sooner. When I heard you were coming to New York, I told Subhash to bring his boys right away."

Daya coughed in surprise. She glared at Subhash and Rohit in turn, then set her glass down firmly. Sahil cautioned her again by shaking his head. "I will marry if and when I want to," she said deliberately, "and my parents will have *no say* in it. I don't need Indians meddling in my private life."

"Ah," Subhash nodded. "A modern girl. And how do you propose to find a man on your own?"

Daya narrowed her eyes and sneered, "By kidnapping and raping him, how else?" She cut into her samosa with an exaggerated swing of the knife, then licked the blade clean.

Sahil burst out laughing. Ranjan pushed the food around his plate in embarrassment and the two older men shook their heads grimly. "My god!" cried Rohit. "Quite a sense of humor you have there, young lady!"

Daya gulped down her drink and looked questioningly at Sahil. *Do something!* her eyes challenged him. Sahil shook his head in disbelief and looked away. His foot tapped nervously.

"American-style romance is not for you, my dear," Subhash continued. "You won't like it. These Americans get you undressed, then drop you just like *that!*" Subhash snapped his fingers. "Once an Indian girl's reputation is destroyed, that's the end of her."

"And this kissing thing!" bellowed Rohit. "My god, I hope you're not one of these junglees who likes spit and slobber and stuffing someone's dirty tongue in your mouth. *Chheee!*"

"And then, too, you have to put dangerous chemicals in your body so you don't get pregnant or diseased while you're fooling around. Naturally all of that harms the unborn babies."

"And you, young lady," Rohit pointed vigorously at Daya, "you definitely need to have a baby to round out your sharp edges."

Daya's dropped fork clattered loudly on her plate. She slumped forward in her chair. She felt her throat tightening with rage. *Enjoy yourself...smile...it's just between Indians.* Her mother's parting words echoed deafeningly in her ears.

"Perhaps you shouldn't talk about her like she's not in the room," Sahil cautioned the older men.

Rohit waved aside Sahil's comment. "What's the problem?" he demanded. "In my day, the women used to eat in a separate room. We could talk about whatever we wanted. If she's such a modern girl, let her deal with it. She's too proud to be one of us!"

"So, tell me again what you're doing hanging around with this family?"

Dinner was finally over. Rohit, Subhash and Ranjan had hurried down to the basement to watch sports on the giant screen TV, leaving Daya and Sahil to clear the table.

"On days like this," Sahil replied bitterly, "I really don't know. All three of them should be shot, or castrated, or both."

They stood side by side at the sink. Daya rinsed the plates and handed them to Sahil to place in the dishwasher.

"They're completely fucked up," she said gloomily. "It's really depressing." She pushed the hair out of her eyes. She couldn't handle another meal like this one. She wanted to talk to her parents, but as per their warning, she had to wait for them to call her. Long-distance phone bills were a touchy subject with her parents and their friends.

Sahil wiped his hands on his pants and turned Daya toward him.

"They really hurt you, didn't they? I'm so sorry. I felt like an utter fool sitting there, politely attempting to steer the conversation away."

She shrugged nonchalantly, but her grim face betrayed the pain she felt. "It's only normal. Indian men are like that."

He gently touched her arm. "Don't take it in," he murmured. "Don't let it get to you."

Daya turned back to the dishes in the sink. "I don't need your pity! I'm sure you've never been attacked like this."

"Mmmm. I thought we had joined forces. But here you are dismissing me once again."

Daya rinsed the plates in silence, then turned off the tap. "I've done quite well for myself, thank you, simply by staying away from Indians. No other men seem to have a stake in humiliating me in this way."

"I understand," Sahil nodded. "But I don't like you lumping me with them. I would never humiliate you the way they do. I've suffered at my uncle's hands before."

"And still you come back for more?"

He shrugged and pursed his lips. "Funny thing, this relationship with Uncle. It's because Rohit and Veena have no children of their own. You know how it is."

She shook her head. "No, actually, I don't. Why don't you tell me?"

Sahil thought for a moment. "Ever since my mother died, Rohit and Veena have been our real family. Rohit is a bit out of control; sadistic, even. He can't help it. But he did save our lives."

"You're going to inherit a packet of money, right?" Daya crossed her arms on her chest.

"What?" He was caught off guard. "Oh! Er...some, I'm sure."

"So that's why you put up with Unk."

Sahil's jaw tightened. She knew she had hit a nerve.

"Must be nice being an Indian son. Everyone wants you like you're going out of style!" Daya snapped her fingers and walked out of the kitchen.

"Now Sahil, you're in charge of the burglar alarm. Don't forget to turn it on before going to bed. Good night."

Daya lay on her bed in the dark, listening to Rohit's instructions in the hallway below. She heard him climb the stairs to his bedroom and shut the door. She heard Ranjan leave the bathroom in the hallway. He slowly walked over to Daya's closed door. She could feel him hesitating outside. The floor boards squeaked with his every move. He might even have raised a hand to knock, but then he turned around and walked back to the room he was sharing with Subhash. He shut his door.

Gathering courage, Daya thought idly, staring at the ceiling. Her parents had not called. Risking their wrath she had tried their number, but there was no answer. *Probably out to a lavish family dinner, celebrating the double pregnancies of their young brides or something.*

It was up to Daya. Should she take up Sahil's offer and go stay with his friends? Or should she stay in the house and go on the attack against the men? She had visions of grabbing Ranjan by his crotch and forcing him to his knees, while his father and uncle pleaded for his life. She imagined grabbing Sahil in the same way and suddenly felt hot. She pushed the image out of her mind.

Daya was incensed that Rohit had ordered his nephews to fly to New York. But what really made her burn was the realization that her parents must have given their blessings to this matchmaking. She had been unleashed into exactly the kind of situation she feared most. She had been preparing for this betrayal for years, and now the moment was upon her.

Choosing her own boyfriends had not sent a strong enough signal to her parents. They apparently could not let go of the fantasy that their daughter needed an Indian man. And a nephew of Rohit, their old friend! A coup, no less. They would be delirious with excitement if she reported back to her parents that the matchmaking had worked. Overnight, their attitude toward her would change, become more generous, more respectful, more relaxed. Her mother would hover around her, laughing, joking, confiding in her as she prepared Daya for being a wife. *You're lucky,* she might say. *You don't have to deal with a mother-in-law in this case.* Or, *Rohit and Veena are wealthy. They will buy you everything, starting with your very own house!* And perhaps even, *Make sure and use birth control so that you can finish your studies in peace. Don't have any children until you're ready to, otherwise it will be the end.* On and on went the imagined dialogues in her head. Fantasizing intimate moments with her mother was something Daya could do for hours. Finally, she sat up and massaged her tense shoulders. *I need to look at this differently,* she cautioned herself. *Because I know I'm not about to get married.*

The thought of another gin and tonic felt good. She put on her clothes and shoes. She hoped Rohit didn't lock the liquor cabinet at night the way her parents did. She walked noiselessly down the stairs to the kitchen. The kitchen door was closed, the same way it had been earlier that day. What a nightmare of a day it had been. She pulled angrily on the door. It swung open silently. She walked right to the liquor cabinet and, with the help of the pale moonlight, located the bottle of gin. She opened the refrigerator and pulled out a bottle of tonic water and a tray of ice. In the vegetable bin she found half a lime.

She quickly poured her drink over the ice, squeezed in the lime and sucked on her wet fingers. She shut the refrigerator door, and walked towards the kitchen table, sipping on her drink. She stopped short, the hair rising on her arms. Her throat tightened with the now familiar anger.

"You've come to join me." Sahil's warm voice floated over to Daya.

Sahil's legs were stretched out on the tabletop and his hands were tucked behind his head. His silk shirt was open to the waist and his sleeves rolled up almost to his shoulders.

"Sorry," Daya said coldly. "I didn't know you were in here."

She stood for a moment, undecided. Should she take her drink up to the room? The room was like a prison. Better just to stay and talk to him. In the light of the moon, the hair on Sahil's chest glinted silver.

"You're catching a moon tan?" she asked dryly as she sat down.

"The truth is, I'm always warm in this house," he grinned. "*Hot*, actually."

She sipped on her drink then pushed the glass across the table to Sahil. "Have a sip," she offered. "Cool yourself down."

He drank out of the glass, then pressed its cool surface against his forehead.

"Do you come here often?"

"Third time this year."

"All because your dad wants to move to New York?"

Sahil looked up in surprise, then smiled knowingly. "Is that what Ranjan's been telling you? We have no intention of moving here. It's just that Rohit has been very active in searching out a wife for Ranjan."

"Just for Ranjan? What about you?"

"Ranjan's older, so he goes first."

"Yeah, but after he's found one, you'll want one too. That's how brothers are."

Sahil nodded noncommittally.

"So," Daya snorted. "I'm the third guinea pig this year?"

Sahil tapped on the table with his fingertips. "You really mustn't be Indian. You seem to have nothing but contempt for family obligations."

"It's only fitting," she murmured, "since Indian families show little more than contempt for their daughters."

She took a gulp of her drink. "Were you sitting here thinking about your mother?"

He took the glass from her hands and looked into the liquid. He ran his finger dejectedly around the rim of the glass. Daya sensed an overwhelming sadness in him and felt sorry.

"You don't have to answer that," she murmured.

"Actually, I was. It happened twenty years ago, you know, in this house."

"What!" Daya started in her chair. "Here? In this house?"

He nodded. "Right here."

She felt her stomach muscles knotting with shock. "I don't understand why no one's ever told me about this."

"Oh, they never talk about it. Ever."

Sahil paused.

"My mother killed herself when I was six. I was at the super-market with Veena. Rohit was at work. Dad was in Africa."

Daya forced her eyes to stay open, forced her ears to listen. "She had planned to take Ranjan with her, to heaven, according to him. She didn't want *me*, again according to him. At the last minute, Ranjan ran from her bedroom. She had already swallowed all the pills. She called for him but he wouldn't go to her. She called for him again and again, but you see, Ranjan refused to go without...," his voice broke. He swallowed and coughed. "He...wouldn't...go...without...me. He's alive today because of...of me."

Daya watched as Sahil locked and unlocked his fingers in quick jerking movements. In the darkness his hands rose and subsided like netted birds. Slowly, she placed her hand on top of his. He exhaled loudly and squeezed her hand gratefully. "Quite frankly, Ranjan has never recovered. He's still afraid...he doesn't trust women...he has nightmares that any wife of his..." He shook his head sadly.

"Oh no! Why is he insisting on getting married, then?"

Sahil chuckled, despite himself. "He's thirty years old. He's never been with a woman. He's right on the edge!"

Daya pressed her lips together grimly. "I was right the first time. Someone should get him to a prostitute."

He patted her hand and pulled away. "My brother won't find Mum in a whorehouse." He tucked his hands back behind his head.

"I'm sorry," she mumbled. "I feel so stupid. I wish I'd known earlier. I feel bad about the way I treated your brother...I...I'm sure I would have been more sensitive if I'd known..."

Sahil flashed her a wry smile. "But I've enjoyed every minute of your headstrong company. You're...you're so *committed* to life."

She felt the hair rise alarmingly on the back of her neck. "Is that...," she began hesitantly. "Is that what you're trying to determine? Which women might kill themselves?"

He looked at her blankly. His breathing slowed. His forehead shone with perspiration. He licked his dry lips, and wiped the sweat off his face. "I suppose I am," he admitted finally. "I've never framed it quite like that before." He struggled for a moment before adding, "But I know you're right."

"And this has only to do with *Indian* women?"

He nodded, brows knit with pain. The conversation was over.

The kitchen clock rang loudly. Daya looked up. It was four A.M. She stood up from the table. Immediately Sahil got to his feet and came around. She knew instinctively what he would do next, and the anticipation of his touch carried her forward into Sahil's embrace.

They walked side by side up the stairs. At the door to her room, they embraced once more. Daya stepped into her room and shut the door quietly. She slid under the covers and sank into sleep.

"So how many other eligible girls have slept in my bed?"

"A few, but we've changed the sheets since then!"

Daya and Ranjan sat at a corner table in the dimly lit Victoria Palace. The restaurant was furnished like a Victorian doll house, with ruffled curtains on the windows, candy-stripe wallpaper and pink and white chairs with high backs. The waiters wore formal tails and high-collared shirts. The menu consisted entirely of meat dishes. Ranjan had insisted that she order a filet mignon or at least a rack of lamb. Ranjan meanwhile had ordered only a baked potato and a salad for himself. She found the situation extremely funny, and Ranjan was relaxed because Daya was having a good time.

Daya had awoken late that morning with the clear knowledge that she should accept Ranjan's invitation to lunch. She had dressed and descended the stairs, and much to her relief, Ranjan was the only one around. He was in the kitchen, and got up hurriedly when Daya walked in. Ranjan was sure that she would shout at him again. He almost burst into tears when instead Daya said she'd be happy to have lunch with him. But there was one condition, she had informed him: they had to speak honestly about themselves.

"Why are you so sure you want to marry an Indian woman? Are they somehow better than other women?" Daya popped another piece of red meat into her mouth, savoring the tenderness.

"I think so," Ranjan answered. "And anyway," he blushed

visibly and concentrated on his salad, "they're the most beautiful women in the world."

"You think?" she asked with surprise. "Funny. I feel the same way. Those big dark eyes and lips..."

"You're extremely attractive," Ranjan interrupted quickly. "And rather intelligent. I saw that at once."

Daya smiled kindly and touched his hand.

"I'm not the one for you," she stated. "Don't waste your time."

Ranjan nodded silently and picked at his salad.

"Do you like my brother?" he asked, still looking at his plate.

She sighed and wondered how to answer.

"Your brother isn't looking for a wife. It...makes things a little easier between us."

Ranjan pushed the lettuce around his plate.

"He's stolen every girl I've been interested in. Once they meet him, they won't have anything to do with me. It's not fair."

Daya frowned impatiently.

"That doesn't sound like your brother. Where are these girls? What happened to them?"

"I don't know. He doesn't tell me anything. All I know is that he slept with Rachna, my...my...the girl I was engaged to."

Oh no, she groaned to herself. *More intrigue. These two are obsessed with each other.*

"Why are you telling me this?" Daya asked in irritation. "She obviously never loved you."

"She didn't love Sahil either," Ranjan cried bitterly. "But she slept with him and not me!"

Daya felt a headache coming on. She was still exhausted from the previous night. The steak sat heavily in her stomach. She suddenly wanted to lie down.

"Let's go," she said tiredly, pushing her plate away. "I feel terrible. I need a rest."

"Won't you finish your steak?" Ranjan blurted in a panic. "You don't have to waste good food on my account."

When Daya opened her eyes, it was dark outside. She was surprised. Her watch read 10:40 P.M. She had slept right through dinner! *Well, no big loss,* she thought, *the boys can manage their soap opera without me.* She smelled the armpit of her t-shirt. The sour smell reminded her immediately of her lunch with Ranjan. She sat up and reached for her jeans in the dark.

"You're awake." Sahil's soft voice floated up through the darkness.

Daya jumped off the bed in fright, clutching her pants to her body.

"What are you doing here?" she hissed. "*Why* are you here?" As her eyes adjusted, she saw Sahil was sitting on the floor by the dresser. "How long have you been sitting there?"

"Not long," Sahil smiled. "I didn't want to go to bed without seeing you. There's been a change in our plan and we're leaving early in the morning."

"Oh?" Daya quickly pulled on her jeans and shirt and sat on the bed. "Where are you going?"

"Home. To London."

"Why so suddenly?" Daya asked, irritated. "Is there a girl waiting for Ranjan?"

Sahil chuckled and stood up. "There could be, for all I know. We have relatives coming in from India. From my mother's side. We haven't seen them in years."

"You're looking forward to meeting them?" Daya asked with disbelief.

"I am, actually. They've always spoiled us rotten. My gran's a brilliant cook, and full of funny stories."

"About your mother?" Daya interjected.

"Yes, but so much more. She's as solid as a rock."

Daya looked at the ceiling, struggling with a sense of sadness.

"I'll miss you," she said finally. Sahil squatted at the foot of the bed.

"I was just thinking the same thing," he murmured. "I feel happy with you. Light. Something's opened up in me." Sahil ran a finger between Daya's toes and her foot jerked back.

"You're ticklish?" Sahil grinned.

"Very," Daya whispered hoarsely. She stopped herself from adding, *Except when I'm aroused.*

Daya and Sahil looked at each other. Sahil's jaw was tense. His amber eyes shone eerily like cat's eyes in the moonlight. Daya swallowed hard. Her chest was so tight it hurt.

"Aren't your relatives wondering where you are?" Daya drew her legs under her and leaned back.

"Even if they knew, they would never come in here."

"Why? Are they all afraid of you?"

Sahil opened his palms to her and motioned for her to extend her legs. "No, that's not it," he replied. Daya unfolded her legs and wiggled her toes. Sahil caught hold of them and pulled her down the bed. He cradled one foot in his palms and put his mouth on her small toe. The intensity of his touch shot through Daya like a spark. She gripped the side of the mattress. Sahil switched to the next toe and Daya bit her lip to keep from crying out. She willed her body to relax, willed the surface tickling to move deeper, down, down into her belly where it flared and burned slowly.

She lay quieter, allowing Sahil's tongue to stroke her feet, arousing her. Her face felt hot, as though she had just sneezed. *Even if it's just once,* she said to herself, *I want him.*

Daya unbuttoned her jeans and pulled her t-shirt over her head. Sahil carefully eased her jeans and underpants off her body. He kissed her ankle and licked up the side of one leg, all the way up inside her thigh and then back down the other until he was at her toes again. Daya felt her body shivering in response. She watched Sahil licking and massaging her feet. His head was bent over in deep concentration. Daya wiggled her toes and Sahil looked up.

"Hi," she greeted him softly, her voice thick with arousal.

Sahil threw off his clothes and climbed over Daya. His entire body was covered with the thick soft hair that covered his chest. Daya pulled Sahil to her and they embraced in a long luxurious hug.

"It's so good to be holding you at last," Sahil whispered, running his fingers through her hair. "I've been sitting on an erection for an hour!" he laughed. "I tried talking to it, but it knew better."

Daya reached down with her hand. Sahil dug his face into her neck and bit her earlobe. Daya struggled out of his grasp and pinned his arms back against the headboard. She straddled him and sucked hard on his left nipple, feeling it stiffen. His body spasmed as she ran the edge of her teeth across the rigid flesh.

"Christ," he sighed happily. "You're a tigress."

"And you," she teased, "are not Indian."

Sahil pulled her face up to his and kissed her. He buried his mouth in her armpit and she pressed him hard against her to keep from crying out.

"You smell so good," he whispered between strokes of his tongue. "I want to taste you, put my mouth on you."

He slid down the bed. She guided his hand between her legs, then his head. He tasted her flesh with long strokes of his tongue. She closed her legs around his head.

"Has anyone told you what you taste like?" he asked, raising his head to look at her.

Daya smiled at him lazily.

"Tuna fish?" she asked jokingly.

Sahil shook his head vehemently.

"The cream inside a freshly cut lady finger," he corrected her solemnly. Daya gaped at him.

"Lady finger? You mean, okra?" She shook with silent laughter.

"A vegetarian right down to the sex!"

Daya awoke with a start. Dawn was just breaking. She could hear footsteps on the staircase, and then below in the front room. She remembered that the London Patels were leaving that morning. She remembered her time with Sahil. The events of the previous night rushed through her head. She relived their tenderness together over and over in her mind. She felt exhausted and alive. Sahil had told her before leaving that she need not wake up to say goodbye in the morning. It would be awkward to exchange mere formalities after being so intimate together. She heard the car start, heard the car doors open and shut, and then the car drive away.

Daya looked out at the rising sun. It felt like the sun was setting already, the end of a long day. It was time to go back to sleep, to get some rest. She wondered if there was another pillow in the room. She looked around. There was a wardrobe next to the chest of drawers into which she had thrown her clothes. She climbed out of bed and pulled on the door of the wardrobe. It wouldn't open. *Great,* she thought. *Like good Indians, the Patels keep all their cupboards locked.* She pulled again on the door. This time the door opened a crack.

She pried the door open with her nails. The hinges moaned as she pushed each door to its limit. Folded neatly and hung on thick steel hangers were dozens of saris. She ran her fingers along the folds. She could tell immediately from the designs that the saris were dated: they were chiffons with loud multicolored geometrical designs. Late '60s or early '70s. She smiled. Veena Auntie must have saved all her old saris, loathe to throw them out. Daya's mother was the same way, with piles of saris that she refused to wear but was unwilling to give away. At the end of the row of saris hung a dozen or so sari blouses of different colors. Daya disliked saris, but loved the blouses for the midriffs they so wonderfully bared. She pulled out a green silk blouse and held it against her. It looked like it might fit. She imagined Sahil's fingers slowly undoing each hook that ran down the front of the blouse. She wanted to feel the soft material against her flesh. She pulled the blouse off the hanger. Was Veena really that thin in those days? A label sewn onto the inside of the blouse caught her eye. Similar white labels were sewn into every one of her mother's blouses. They had all been stitched in India.

Daya read the label, Manjuri S. Patel. Manjuri? She wondered who that could be...S. The middle initial stood for the husband's first name in the full name of a married Indian woman. S...could be S for Subhash...

Daya threw the blouse onto the bed. *It can't be! It can't be.* She looked around her at the walls of the bedroom. There were water stains on the ceiling. There were cobwebs in the corner. The window sills were caked with dust.

Suddenly Sahil's words hit her in the face.

"They would never come in here."

Daya flung open the door and leaped out of the room before she realized she was naked. She stepped back into the room and grabbed her clothes off the floor. Her hands were shaking. Her legs got stuck in the jeans. She pulled them on with sheer force. Her arms were sweating. They got stuck in the sleeves of her t-shirt and she pulled the shirt roughly over her head. She ran into Rohit's bedroom, picked up the phone, and asked the operator to call her home collect. Her mother answered. The operator asked if she would accept the charges.

"I'm sorry but Daya is not home right now!"

Daya listened to her mother's vigorous denial to the operator. This was the arranged system to signal she wanted her parents to call back. Daya hung up the phone and waited. She looked around Rohit's room. The neatness of the room made her want to throw things about, empty the cupboards and dresser onto the floor, splash perfume and aftershave on the walls. A minute passed and the phone remained silent.

Mother! fumed Daya. *For god's sake take this seriously and call now. Not after you finish your conversation, not after you finish your cooking. Now!*

Another minute passed.

Betrayed again and again. Lies everywhere. Who was to blame?

The phone rang. Daya snatched it off the cradle furiously.

"Why the hell must you take so long to return my call? First of all you promised to call the day I arrived. Today is the third day. What excuse could you possibly have? You have no sense of time once your darling sons arrive in the house. I could have been killed by now!"

There was silence on the other end. Daya couldn't believe her mother's callousness.

"Do I mean so little to you? Did you have any thoughts for my feelings when you set me up with these morbid nephews of Rohit's? What in hell was going through your mind? Do you have any idea what sickos the two brothers are? Answer me, mother! I have a right to know." Daya fought back the tears of rage that choked her throat.

"Daya, sweetheart, is that you?" Her mother's voice sounded strange, differently pitched, very far away. "It's me, Auntie Veena, calling from Bombay. What is going on? What have those two naughty boys done now?" Daya pulled the receiver away from her ear.

Oh no, Veena! Not now. Where were you when I needed you?

"Daya!" Veena cried urgently. "Speak to me. Are you all right? Did they hurt you? Isn't your uncle around? Talk to him, darling, tell him everything. He loves you like a father. Daya, answer me!"

Daya felt the tears burning her face. *Why? Why in his mother's deathbed?*

"Sweetheart, those two boys are basically good at heart. They would never do anything to hurt you. Whatever happened, happened. Let it be now, let it go. I'm sorry I called when you were expecting your mother, but I'm sure she would say exactly what I'm telling you. You're young still, you have your whole life ahead of you. Forget it ever happened. Daya, are you there?"

She held her hand over her eyes and shook her head slowly.

"It's okay if you can't talk now, darling. I'll be home in two days. Uncle and I will take you out for a nice dinner, and then you can tell us everything..."

Daya put the phone down. Immediately it rang again. She walked into her bedroom, snatched up all her clothes and stuffed them into her bag. She walked down the stairs and out of the house. Daya checked her pocket for change. It would be a dollar or so to get to Manhattan. She should have gone the first day, should have gone and done what she came to do, instead of getting caught up with the men. When she arrived at the bus stop, a bus was pulling up. She asked the driver if he went down Museum Mile and he nodded.

Daya stared out of the window, concentrating on every shop name, every road sign, every hoarding. The intimacies of the night before tumbled through her head. She combed the images one by one to locate even a single dishonest touch, look or action. They had held each other for so long, in so many different ways. Not once had he pulled away from her. Not once had his loving attention flagged.

"Here's where the museums start, miss!" the bus driver called cheerfully to Daya. She sprang out of her seat and hurried off the bus.

Museum Mile on Fifth Avenue. Not a soul on the streets. She had hoped to encounter crowds of people, had envisioned losing herself in the rushing bodies of New Yorkers. She walked quickly. She would tire herself out.

How many women had been condemned to that bed? Daya felt numb with grief. She waited for the familiar anger to rise through her once again, but the memories of the previous night were still locked in her groin, glowing like coals. The warmth in her body moved upward and outward, comforting her. She felt his gentle hands on her face. And it was then that she understood. He'd had to do it. In some strange way, it had broken the spell that hung over him.

She walked past a hot dog vendor. He had big drooping eyes, chubby jowls and a bushy mustache. He looked Greek. He caught her eye and waved enthusiastically. His gaze was inquiring. Two blocks down he was there again. "You are Greek?" he shouted, arms in the air. "Come, come!"

Daya walked on.

"Armenian? Turkish? Palestinian?" he called frantically. She ducked into a museum.

The security guard at the museum addressed her before she had even crossed the gate. "I am from Guyana. You are also from Guyana?"

"No!" Daya snapped at the guard and rushed in.

"Trinidad? Jamaica? Fiji?" he called after her. "I'm sure I know you!"

Daya didn't know what museum she had walked into. There were old oil paintings in heavy gold frames. They were portraits of pale people, with faces brightly lit; the rest of their bodies were in darkness. The faces were expressionless and looked like they had been painted off cadavers. She decided to leave through a side exit, to avoid another encounter with the security guard.

As she pushed open the door, the hot dog vendor was right there again. He opened his hands wide and pleaded with her. "You are Lebanese? Egyptian? Iraqi? Come, come, I feed you!"

She frowned at him and turned away. The hot dog vendor followed at a trot, and walked alongside her. "Very nice!" he smiled, framing Daya's face in the air. "Woman," he added emphatically, "where you from?"

Daya stopped and scowled at him.

"Isn't it *obvious* that I'm Indian?"

The hot dog vendor clapped his hands.

"Ah, Indian!" he repeated with delight. "India! Most beautiful woman in India. Most wonderful woman in India. I see movies. Happy, happy, dancing, singing!" The Greek sprang from leg to leg and snapped his fingers in the air.

"Every man love Indian woman! Whole world love Indian woman!"

Daya took a long look at the singing shaking jowls and the merry twinkling eyes. She started laughing. This man was insane. Stark raving mad.

The Greek danced toward her, then away from her, then whirled around and around, encircling her. She watched the man through tired eyes. She drew in deep gulps of the warm spring air. "Beautiful, beautiful Indian woman! Happy, happy Indian woman!" The Greek danced on, lost in his hymns of praise.

Daya watched him shout out his joy.

This is what I came for, this is what brought me here.

When he finally stopped, she clapped for him. He came up to her and saluted her, bowing low to the ground. Daya shook his hand. "Thanks for the reminder," she said softly.

The Greek smiled at her, not understanding. He snapped his fingers and leapt in the air one last time, then retreated to his hot dog stand. Daya waved to the Greek, but his back was turned to her as he resumed pushing his cart down the street.

So many years of anger, Daya mused, *and this man sees only beauty in my face.* She looked at her reflection in the window of the museum. Her smiling eyes shone back at her, gleaming with a mischievous light.

The Smell

"Aren't you going to vomit now?" I prodded my cousin Nila.

"No, why should I?" She looked at me from the corner of her eye as she carefully tied my new chiffon scarf around her head. We were in the hallway right outside B.A.'s room, where she was taking her afternoon nap. The door to her room was partially open and I could see my grandmother's stout old body curled up on the narrow bed.

"If you don't vomit yourself, I'll make you." I jabbed my finger into Nila's side and she bent forward, giggling.

"But how can I vomit just like that? Have some sense. I can't just tell my stomach, now please vomit." Nila laughed as she whirled in front of the mirror, caressing the silky scarf from Hong Kong.

"You ate meat." I growled. "Now don't you want to?"

"When did I eat meat! I'm not like you, dirty girl. I'm a hundred percent vegetarian." Nila's voice always rose sharply on the words *hundred percent vegetarian*. She had heard that my branch of the family ate dirty things like chicken and mutton and...*god-knows-what-else!*

In her room, B.A. stirred and smacked her lips, pulling the pillow down over her ears.

"I just fed you some, stupid. Now vomit."

"What do you mean? You gave me a...a...what do you call it..."

"Ya, but you know the soft pink part in the middle? That was egg and meat. *Chicken's* egg and *cow's* meat. *Raw.*"

At the mention of cow's meat, Nila's throat tightened and she made a faint retching sound. She thought for a moment, then shook her head firmly.

"How can there be meat inside a sweet? You must be mad," she offered bravely, but already her hands were nervously massaging her throat.

"Did I make it? How would I know why there's meat inside a sweet! But you ate it, and I'm going to tell B.A., and she will hit you. You might as well vomit now, so there won't be any beating."

Nila looked around her and suddenly realized that we were standing right outside B.A.'s room. Her eyes widened and her face lengthened fearfully. She clapped her hand over her mouth, but, too late, the pink mash bubbled out of her and slithered out of her palm.

"Oh god! Oh god, it's coming up...hunnh...uuugggh...uuunnhhh...Mummmeeeeee!"

I flicked the chiffon scarf onto her shoulders, then pushed her head down and away so that I would be spared the disgusting faces she made when she vomited.

"Good, good, good. Mummy's little darling really knows how to make a mess!" I congratulated.

"Mummeeee!" she howled between waves of retching.

"Stop shouting. Your mummy's not here. Just stand quietly next to your precious vomit. The smell of the meat will reach B.A. soon enough and she will come out and see what a good girl you are to vomit it all out. Then she'll put you in her lap and tell you lots of stories and feed you lots of sweets and then before you know it you'll be married off to some oily-pooh. Bye!"

I pulled my new chiffon scarf off Nila's neck and peeped into B.A.'s room. B.A. was sitting up, confused by all the noise. She yawned, drawing in a lungful of air. Suddenly she choked, and thrust her white sari over her nose and mouth. She staggered to her feet and came barreling towards the door. I gleefully slapped Nila on her back, then skipped backward into the kitchen.

"But Rani, I don't *want* to get married. I want to play with you!" Nila sobbed, shaking off the sticky strings that hung from her hand to the floor. A second later, B.A. had a firm grip on Nila's shoulder and was bellowing for the servant to bring sawdust and a broom.

I ran out the other kitchen entrance, and skipped past B.A., well out of her reach. I sang out to Nila. "You silly goose, girls who don't eat meat *always* get married. Bye-bye Mrs. Oily-Pooh!"

Wooden buildings are good for hearing grandmothers slowly climbing up step after step, across the landing and up the next set of stairs. In a wooden house, anyone can hear where anyone else is, if you concentrate hard enough.

Here she comes now. I know how many steps; we all do. She groans at every four steps. Between the twelfth and thirteenth steps, she burps long, like a donkey braying. Fifteen steps to clear the landing, then onto the next set of steps. We live on the third floor. She lives on the ground floor. Every morning she climbs up those steps and landings to come and sniff for eggs.

Most grandmothers don't like playing games with children, but our B.A. is different. Every morning she plays this game with us. She wants to. No one forces her. She does her round every morning, like a baby or a puppy who can play games only one way.

As soon as we hear the first thump on the wooden steps, we move quickly to the back of the kitchen. We run into the servants' room and close the door. Then the fun begins.

First, the cook turns on the burner, throws a spoonful of ghee into the pan and heats it on the flame.

The first groan signals she has covered four steps.

The ghee melts and bubbles. The cook quickly breaks the eggs on the side of the pan and pours them in. The heat of the pan sends clouds of egg steam rushing around the room, filling every corner.

The donkey bray warns us that she's near the first landing. She clumps across.

My brother lifts his head and pushes up his eyeglasses. He opens the packet of bread wrapped in wax paper and pulls out four slices, two for him and two for me. The eggs are fried for just a few seconds and then the cook drops the bread into the pan as well.

B.A. is across the first landing and on the second set of stairs.

The cook presses the bread into the ghee, presses it flat until the slices have become crisp brown pancakes. We've told him that we like our eggs *on toast*, and this is the only way to make toast in the servants' room. In this way, the bread supports the eggs without getting soggy. The cook slides the fried eggs onto the fried bread and lifts the food onto our plates.

B.A. crosses the second landing. She brays out of turn, and we freeze. Have we miscalculated? But it is a false alarm.

My brother and I attack the eggs on toast with huge bites. Four steps up for grandma, four bites for the two of us, and the first of the eggs are gone. The windows of the room are shut to keep the breeze from blowing out the burner flame. The smell of eggs is very strong.

Why don't you ever come to see me, why do you avoid me, huh? What kind of children are you, ignoring an old woman like me, why don't you come and greet me every morning, I don't take up much time in your day. All day long you play as much as you want, don't you? Is five minutes so precious that you can't stop and come see me? I don't hit you; I don't say bad things about you. I don't say anything about the fancy clothes you wear or the expensive foreign chocolates your mummy and daddy feed you. I just want you to come see me. Just touch my feet quickly and tell me some sweet things and then you can go on your way. All day long my feet hurt me, my back hurts me, my hair falls out and my stomach falls in. Do you ever stop to think that a little love would cure my pain? You only think bad thoughts about me and come to my room only when you're forced to. Is this any way to treat your old grandmother?

We gobble up the remaining food. We open the windows in the

servants' room. *Whoooshhh!* The breeze blows in and magically the smell of eggs is gone. My brother burps. Out comes egg smell. I hold my breath and burp even longer and harder. Out comes double-powered egg smell. *Whooooshhh!* The breeze blows it all away. I look at my brother with disappointment. It's going to be just another morning, and B.A. won't sniff out the eggs today.

Kesho? Rani? Where are you my darlings? Come and touch the feet of your grandmother, you little rascals! Come to me while you're still clean, before the dirt of the whole world covers you from head to toe! Dirty rascals, playing in god knows what room with who knows what filthy people!

We open the door of the servants' room with sour faces. B.A. stares at us. She has a round wrinkled face and wears round thick glasses. She is as wide as she is tall. At her full height she is no taller than a child. She wears the same white sari every day. She is confused every day about why we are in the servants' room. She asks us with contempt:

What are you doing? Who let you in there? You should be in your own room. How many times have I told your father that you shouldn't be alone with servants! I can't imagine what all goes on behind my back.

The cook is already squatting over the sunken toilet inside the servants' room, scrubbing out the fried-egg pan with mud and ashes. He washes the pan in this way every day, balancing precariously over the oval porcelained opening. Water dribbles out of a rusty faucet which is connected to a thin water pipe that pokes through the ceiling. The cook is used to washing up in this way because the toilet serves as the servants' bathing area as well.

You, you…good-for-nothing cook! How many times have I told you that the children don't belong in this part of the house? Ehh? You'll turn them into useless beggars like yourself! Have you no shame? These are children of good family.

B.A. leans right into the bathroom, holding onto the door and covering her nose with the end of her sari. The cook glares at her and stands up, shaking the beads of water off the clean frying pan. B.A. shrinks back as the cook pushes past her. He snaps at her.

Am I the owner of this house? Are these my children? Tie them up if you don't want them in here!

B.A.'s nostrils flare in alarm. She bends forward, sniffing madly.

Something is wrong here. Somebody is eating something that we do not allow in this house.

B.A. can smell something like the odor of meat on the cook.

It's him! He stinks of meat! Oh god, oh god, oh god! This is how we live in Bombay, suffering the sins of our servants. Kesho? Rani? Come here at once! I will say a prayer for you.

B.A. pulls us close and then pushes us away. She starts sniffing again. She brushes off our school clothes to get the cook's smell off. Still she sniffs. Her lips quiver with anger and her eyes open wide. I taunt her before she can speak.

Do you want me to vomit? I'll do it right now, right here. Then you can see for yourself what I've eaten. Don't you want me to?

B.A. is suddenly confused by my offer. I sound too eager. There appears to be no punishment in it for me. She sighs and smiles sadly.

No, no, you mustn't get yourself dirty. You have to go to school now. You must hurry down to the car, no?

We nod vigorously, wave to B.A., pick up our book bags and run to the stairs. I race my brother down, laughing and pushing. He lets me win because, once again, I have challenged B.A. and won at her daily morning game.

On my cousin Sonia's wedding day, she couldn't stop vomiting. No one could understand what it was. Did she have a fever, were there worms in her system, had she eaten some rotten food? No, no, no, she shook her head. The vomiting kept her so busy that she couldn't even talk. Even after there was nothing left in her stomach, she kept heaving and crying.

Her parents went to B.A. What are we to do? This girl can hardly walk into the marriage tent. She will surely faint while the priest performs the service. How will it look? What will people think?

B.A. dismissed them with contempt. There is nothing wrong with Sonia, she scolded. The problem was with the *groom*, who smelled of meat!

B.A.'s strict training of the girls in the house had made its mark. Sonia was sensitive to the smell of strangers. B.A. telephoned the groom's house, where they were just preparing to leave. Under pressure from B.A., the groom's father admitted that his son did occasionally eat meat. B.A. tearfully announced the news.

Sonia lifted her aching body off the floor and stood tall and proud like a warrior queen. She lifted her hand imperially and her parents stepped back in fear. With the clear voice of conviction, Sonia shouted that under no circumstances would she marry a sinful, polluted, meat-eating man!

Immediately her mother started weeping. Her father's legs gave out from under him and he crumpled to the floor. Sonia stood with her hands on her hips and her legs firmly planted, daring any family member to challenge her.

I was thrilled! My cousin was refusing marriage! Finally, we would have a real rebel in the house. I was delirious with excitement, hopping from foot to foot and swallowing my laughter in great gulps. Sonia was my new hero.

But then Sonia's father called in the priest for a hurried discussion. A few phone calls were made, and within the hour, a hundred-percent-vegetarian groom was found for the bride. Sonia checked carefully with the priest, and then spoke to the vegetarian groom's parents and grandparents, friends and neighbors, and then touched the feet of the priest and agreed that the marriage would proceed.

I was in shock. Sonia had betrayed me. How could she turn her back on freedom? Her warrior stance collapsed once more into the frightened nervous hunch that had always marked her posture. I blamed B.A. for making Sonia into a robot. I sat outside the marriage tent for the entire ceremony and never even saw the face of the groom.

Now Sonia and her husband live somewhere far away and I haven't seen my cousin since. But I hear every now and then that even with a vegetarian husband, Sonia vomits every day. She smells meat everywhere, all the time. Her husband beats her daily because she won't let him touch her. She can't get rid of the smell.

B.A. no longer says anything about her, in fact no one is allowed to say anything about Sonia. If B.A. finds us talking, she'll just make us vomit all the words out.

Rani! Always remember, if anyone ever feeds you anything that looks, or smells, or tastes non-vegetarian, just vomit it out! Don't even think about it, just do it. You are a child still, so it will come to you naturally. Every good girl can vomit. I know, because when I was given bad food in the house of bad people, I vomited. It was very easy. I stayed clean, clean, clean. In my days in the village, it didn't happen very often. But these days, in a place like Bombay, even decent people might trick you. Eating meat is not good for women. Unnecessarily you will pollute your unborn son. You listen to your B.A. Anytime I say to you, Spit it out, you must do so automatically or you will go to hell.

Rani! Did you hear what I just said? You better stay clean, or no one is going to marry their son to you! You best listen to your B.A., or you'll end up a dried-up old hag and no one will pay any attention to you.

Sometimes the cook brings home mutton kheema wrapped in a banana leaf and packed in newspaper. I sit with the cook in the servants' room as he deftly scoops up the meat with pieces of white bread and gobbles down mouthful after mouthful. I draw the mutton smell into my nose with long breaths that fill me up. I exhale reluctantly. I arrange a line of the spicy ground meat along my finger so that it resembles a moist dark caterpillar. I lick at it slowly. When we have finished eating, I run my finger through the small pool of grease collected on the banana leaf and coat it thoroughly with the red oil. I spread the oil on my wrist and then go find my brother. I brush up against him "accidentally," and smear the mutton oil on his arm. My brother doesn't even know what I'm doing. I sit next to him as he does his homework or reads a comic book or plays with his trains. He likes my company. The aroma lingers in the air for a long time. Eventually the flies come and start bothering us. Then I grab a blanket or a towel and hug my brother tightly until the oil is wiped away. My brother doesn't know what I'm doing, but he doesn't mind because he likes this game that we play. He smells good and makes my mouth water and I am happy that I can love him in this special way.

When I grow up, I will never vomit. When I grow up, I will never marry. When I grow up I will smell the meat on men and the smell will keep me hungry.

Glossary

Biscuit aapu?	Shall I give you a biscuit?
amma	mother
arrey	exclamation, interjection
ayah	maid
B. Comm.	Bachelor of Commerce
ba	grandmother
baba	father; exclamation similar to "Oh man"
bai	maid
bhabhi	sister-in-law
bhagwan	god
bhajans	hymns
bindi	red dot worn on forehead by married women
brahmin	priest; highest Hindu caste
chai	tea
chapati	flat bread
chhaprasi	sweeper
chuddis	panties
coir	fibers from coconut shell
dhoti	loin cloth
ghee	clarified butter
goonda	thug
hijra	transsexual
Hindi	national language of India
Jain	religious minority; religion stressing nonviolence
junglee	from the jungle, wild
kheema	minced meat
Konkani	language spoken on the western coast of India
memsahib	ma'am
Nanima	affectionate term for 'grandmother'
paise	coins
Parvati	goddess; wife of Shiva

prasad	food blessed by the gods
pukka	real, authentic
puri-bhaji	fried puffed bread and potato vegetable
Ram	incarnation of Lord Vishnu; hero of epic Ramayana
sadhu	holy men who have renounced all things worldly
sahib	sir
salwar-khameez	long tunic worn with loose pants
samosa	fried snack
Satyavan	mythological hero
Savitri	sacrificed herself to save Satyavan
Shiva	Lord of Creation and Destruction
Sita	self-sacrificing wife of Ram
Suitwallah	one who wears a suit
thali	rimmed metal plate

Ginu Kamani was born in Bombay, India, in 1962 and moved to the United States, fourteen years later. Graduating with an M.A. in Creative Writing from the University of Colorado, Boulder in 1987, she returned to Bombay for three years to work in film production, then came back to the U.S. to pursue writing full time. Two of the short stories from this collection and several of her poems were published under her full name, Gaurangi Kamani, in the anthology, *Our Feet Walk the Sky: Women of the South Asian Diaspora* (Aunt Lute, 1993). Kamani, who lives in the Bay Area, is working on film projects while finishing her novel.

aunt lute books is a multicultural women's press that has been committed to publishing high quality, culturally diverse literature since 1982. In 1990, the Aunt Lute Foundation was formed as a non-profit corporation to publish and distribute books that reflect the complex truths of women's lives and the possibilities for personal and social change. We seek work that explores the specificities of the very different histories from which we come, and that examines the intersections between the borders we all inhabit.

Please write or phone for a free catalogue of our other books or if you wish to be on our mailing list for future titles. You may buy books directly from us by phoning in a credit card order or mailing a check with the catalogue order form.

Aunt Lute Books
P. O. Box 410687
San Francisco, CA 94141
(415) 826-1300

This Book would not have been possible without the kind contributions of the *Aunt Lute Founding Friends:*

Anonymous Donor
Anonymous Donor
Rusty Barcelo
Marian Bremer
Diane Goldstein

Diana Harris
Phoebe Robins Hunter
Diane Mosbacher, M.D., Ph.D.
William Preston, Jr.
Elise Rymer Turner